STORIES
&
TEXTS FOR NOTHING

Other Works By Samuel Beckett

Published By Grove Press

Cascando and Other Short Dramatic Pieces

Film

Endgame

Happy Days

How It Is

Krapp's Last Tape and Other Dramatic Pieces

More Pricks Than Kicks

Murphy

Poems in English

Proust

Stories & Texts for Nothing

Molloy

Malone Dies

The Unnamable

Waiting for Godot

Watt

STORIES
&
TEXTS FOR NOTHING

by Samuel Beckett

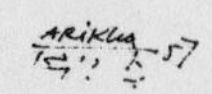

GROVE PRESS, INC. / NEW YORK

Originally published as *Nouvelles et textes pour rien,*
© 1958 by Les Editions de Minuit, Paris, France

The drawings by Avigdor Arikha appeared
in the original French edition

"The Expelled," "The End," and "Texts for Nothing 1"
originally appeared in *Evergreen Review*

Library of Congress Catalog Card Number: 67-20341

Fifth printing

Manufactured in the United States of America

DISTRIBUTED BY RANDOM HOUSE, INC., NEW YORK

CONTENTS

STORIES

THE EXPELLED

There were not many steps. I had counted them a thousand times, both going up and coming down, but the figure has gone from my mind. I have never known whether you should say one with your foot on the sidewalk, two with the following foot on the first step, and so on, or whether the sidewalk shouldn't count. At the top of the steps I fell foul of the same dilemma. In the other direction, I mean from top to bottom, it was the same, the word is not too strong. I did not know where to begin nor where to end, that's the truth of the matter. I arrived therefore at three totally different figures, without ever knowing which of them was right. And when I say that the figure has gone from my mind, I mean that none of the three figures is with me any more, in my mind. It is true that if I were to find, in my mind, where it is certainly to be found, one of these figures, I would find it and it alone, without being able to deduce from it the other two. And even were I to recover two, I would not know the third. No, I would have to find all three, in my mind, in order to know all three. Memories are killing. So you must not think of certain things, of those that are dear to you, or rather you must think of them, for if you don't there is the danger of finding them, in your mind, little by little. That is to say, you must think of them for a while, a good while, every day several times a day, until they sink forever in the mud. That's an order.

After all it is not the number of steps that matters. The important thing to remember is that there were not many, and that I have remembered. Even for the child there were not many, compared to other steps he knew, from seeing them every day, from going up and coming down, and from playing on them at knuckle-bones and other games the very names of which he has forgotten. What must it have been like then for the man I had overgrown into?

The fall was therefore not serious. Even as I fell I heard the door slam, which brought me a little comfort, in the midst of my fall. For that meant they were not pursuing me down into the street, with a stick, to beat me in full view of the passers-by. For if that had been their intention they would not have shut the door, but left it open, so that the persons assembled in the vestibule might enjoy my chastisement and be edified. So, for once, they had confined themselves to throwing me out and no more about it. I had time, before coming to rest in the gutter, to conclude this piece of reasoning.

Under these circumstances nothing compelled me to get up immediately. I rested my elbow on the sidewalk, funny the things you remember, settled my ear in the cup of my hand and began to reflect on my situation, notwithstanding its familiarity. But the sound, fainter but unmistakable, of the door slammed again, roused me from my reverie, in which already a whole landscape was taking form, charming with hawthorn and wild roses, most dreamlike, and made me look up in alarm, my hands flat on the sidewalk and my legs braced for flight. But it was merely my hat sailing towards me through the air, rotating as it came. I caught it and put it on. They were most correct, according to their god.

They could have kept this hat, but it was not theirs, it was mine, so they gave it back to me. But the spell was broken.

How describe this hat? And why? When my head had attained I shall not say its definitive but its maximum dimensions, my father said to me, Come, son, we are going to buy your hat, as though it had pre-existed from time immemorial in a pre-established place. He went straight to the hat. I personally had no say in the matter, nor had the hatter. I have often wondered if my father's purpose was not to humiliate me, if he was not jealous of me who was young and handsome, fresh at least, while he was already old and all bloated and purple. It was forbidden me, from that day forth, to go out bareheaded, my pretty brown hair blowing in the wind. Sometimes, in a secluded street, I took it off and held it in my hand, but trembling. I was required to brush it morning and evening. Boys my age with whom, in spite of everything, I was obliged to mix occasionally, mocked me. But I said to myself, It is not really the hat, they simply make merry at the hat because it is a little more glaring than the rest, for they have no finesse. I have always been amazed at my contemporaries' lack of finesse, I whose soul writhed from morning to night, in the mere quest of itself. But perhaps they were simply being kind, like those who make game of the hunchback's big nose. When my father died I could have got rid of this hat, there was nothing more to prevent me, but not I. But how describe it? Some other time, some other time.

I got up and set off. I forget how old I can have been. In what had just happened to me there was nothing in the least memorable. It was neither the cradle nor the grave of anything whatever. Or rather it resembled so many other cradles, so many other graves, that I'm lost. But I don't believe I exaggerate when I say that I was in the prime of life, what I believe is called the full possession of one's faculties. Ah yes, them I possessed all right. I crossed the street and turned back towards the house that had just ejected me, I who never turned back when leaving. How beautiful it was! There were geraniums in the windows. I have brooded over geraniums for years. Geraniums are artful customers, but in the end I was able to do what I liked with them. I have always greatly admired the door of this house, up on top of its little flight of steps. How describe it? It was a massive green door, encased in summer in a kind of green and white striped housing, with a hole for the thunderous wrought-iron knocker and a slit for letters, this latter closed to dust, flies and tits by a brass flap fitted with springs. So much for that description. The door was set between two pillars of the same colour, the bell being on that to the right. The curtains were in unexceptionable taste. Even the smoke rising from one of the chimney-pots seemed to spread and vanish in the air more sorrowful than the neighbours', and bluer. I looked up at the third and last floor and saw my window outrageously open. A thorough cleaning was in full swing. In a few hours they would close the window, draw the curtains and spray the whole place with disinfectant. I knew them. I would have gladly died in that house. In a sort of vision I saw the door open and my feet come out.

I wasn't afraid to look, for I knew they were not spying on me from behind the curtains, as they could have done if they had wished. But I knew them. They had all gone back into their dens and resumed their occupations.

And yet I had done them no harm.

I did not know the town very well, scene of my birth and of my first steps in this world, and then of all the others, so many that I thought all trace of me was lost, but I was wrong. I went out so little! Now and then I would go to the window, part the curtains and look out. But then I hastened back to the depths of the room, where the bed was. I felt ill at ease with all this air about me, lost before the confusion of innumerable prospects. But I still knew how to act at this period, when it was absolutely necessary. But first I raised my eyes to the sky, whence cometh our help, where there are no roads, where you wander freely, as in a desert, and where nothing obstructs your vision, wherever you turn your eyes, but the limits of vision itself. It gets monotonous in the end. When I was younger I thought life would be good in the middle of a plain, and I went to the Lüneburg heath. With the plain in my head I went to the heath. There were other heaths far less remote, but a voice kept saying to me, It's the Lüneburg heath you need. The element lüne must have had something to do with it. As it turned out the Lüneburg heath was most unsatisfactory, most unsatisfactory. I came home disappointed, and at the same time relieved. Yes, I don't know why, but I have never been disappointed, and I often was in the early days, without feeling at the same time, or a moment later, an undeniable relief.

I set off. What a gait. Stiffness of the lower limbs, as if nature had denied me knees, extraordinary splaying of the feet to right and left of the line of march. The trunk, on the contrary, as if by the effect of a compensatory mechanism, was as flabby as an old ragbag, tossing wildly to the unpredictable jolts of the pelvis. I have often tried to correct these defects, to stiffen my bust, flex my knees and walk with my feet in front of one another, for I had at least five or six, but it always ended in the same way, I mean with a loss of equilibrium, followed by a fall. A man must walk without paying attention to what he's doing, as he sighs, and when I walked without paying attention to what I was doing I walked in the way I have just described, and when I began to pay attention I managed a few steps of creditable execution and then fell. I decided therefore to be myself. This carriage is due, in my opinion, in part at least, to a certain leaning from which I have never been able to free myself completely and which left its stamp, as was only to be expected, on my impressionable years, those which govern the fabrication of character, I refer to the period which extends, as far as the eye can see, from the first totterings, behind a chair, to the third form, in which I concluded my studies. I had then the deplorable habit, having pissed in my trousers, or shat there, which I did fairly regularly early in the morning, about ten or half past ten, of persisting in going on and finishing my day as if nothing had happened. The very idea of changing my trousers, or of confiding in mother, who goodness knows asked nothing better than to help me, was unbearable, I don't know why, and till bedtime I dragged on with burning and stinking between my little thighs, or sticking to my bottom, the result of my incontinence. Whence this wary way of walking, with the legs stiff and wide apart, and this desperate rolling of the bust, no doubt intended to put people off the scent, to make them think I was full of gaiety and high spirits, without a care in the world, and to lend plausibility to my explanations concerning my nether rigidity, which I ascribed to hereditary rheumatism. My youthful ardour, in so far as I had any, spent itself in this effort, I became sour and mistrustful, a little before my time, in love with hiding and the prone position. Poor juvenile solutions, explaining nothing. No need then for caution, we may reason on to our heart's content, the fog won't lift.

The weather was fine. I advanced down the street, keeping as close as I could to the sidewalk. The widest sidewalk is never wide enough for me, once I set myself in motion, and I hate to inconvenience strangers. A policeman stopped me and said, The street for vehicles, the sidewalk for pedestrians. Like a bit of Old Testament. So I got back on the sidewalk, almost apologetically, and persevered there, in spite of an indescribable jostle, for a good twenty steps, till I had to fling myself to the ground to avoid crushing a child. He was wearing a little harness, I remember, with little bells, he must have taken himself for a pony, or a Clydesdale, why not. I would have crushed him gladly, I loathe children, and it would have been doing him a service, but I was afraid of reprisals. Everyone is a parent, that is what keeps you from hoping. One should reserve, on busy streets, special tracks for these nasty little creatures, their prams, hoops, sweets, scooters, skates, grandpas, grandmas, nannies, balloons and balls, all their foul little happiness in a word. I fell then, and brought down with me an old lady covered with spangles and lace, who must have weighed about sixteen stone. Her screams soon drew a crowd. I had high hopes she had broken her femur, old ladies break their femur easily, but not enough, not enough. I took advantage of the confusion to make off, muttering unintelligible oaths, as if I were the victim, and I was, but I couldn't have proved it. They never lynch children, babies, no matter what they do they are whitewashed in advance. I personally would lynch them with the utmost pleasure, I don't say I'd lend a hand, no, I am not a violent man, but I'd encourage the others and stand them drinks when it was done. But no sooner had I begun to reel on than I was stopped by a second policeman, similar in all respects to the first, so much so that I wondered whether it was not the same one. He pointed out to me that the sidewalk was for every one, as if it was quite obvious that I could not be assimilated to that category. Would you like me, I said, without thinking for a single moment of Heraclitus, to get down in the gutter? Get down wherever you want, he said, but leave some room for others. If you can't bloody well get about like every one else, he said, you'd do better to stay at home. It was exactly my feeling. And that he should attribute to me a home was no small satisfaction. At that moment a funeral passed, as sometimes happens. There was a great flurry of hats and at the same time a flutter of countless fingers. Personally if I were reduced to making the sign of the cross I would set my heart on doing it right, nose, navel, left nipple, right nipple. But the way they did it, slovenly and wild, he seemed crucified all of a heap, no dignity, his knees under his chin and his hands anyhow. The more fervent stopped dead and muttered. As for the policeman, he stiffened to attention, closed his eyes and saluted. Through the windows of the cabs I caught a glimpse of the mourners conversing with animation, no doubt scenes from the life of their late dear brother in Christ, or sister. I seem to have heard that the hearse trappings are not the same in both cases, but I never could find out what the difference consists in. The horses were farting and shitting as if they were going to the fair. I saw no one kneeling.

But with us the last journey is soon done, it is in vain you quicken your pace, the last cab containing the domestics soon leaves you behind, the respite is over, the bystanders go their ways, you may look to yourself again. So I stopped a third time, of my own free will, and entered a cab. Those I had just seen pass, crammed with people hotly arguing, must have made a strong impression on me. It's a big black box, rocking and swaying on its springs, the windows are small, you curl up in a corner, it smells musty. I felt my hat grazing the roof. A little later I leant forward and closed the windows. Then I sat down again with my back to the horse. I was dozing off when a voice made me start, the cabman's. He had opened the door, no doubt despairing of making himself heard through the window. All I saw was his moustache. Where to? he said. He had climbed down from his seat on purpose to ask me that. And I who thought I was far away already. I reflected, searching in my memory for the name of a street, or a monument. Is your cab for sale? I said. I added, Without the horse. What would I do with a horse? But what would I do with a cab? Could I as much as stretch out in it? Who would bring me food? To the Zoo, I said. It is rare for a capital to be without a Zoo. I added, Don't go too fast. He laughed. The suggestion that he might go too fast to the Zoo must have amused him. Unless it was the prospect of being cabless. Unless it was simply myself, my own person, whose presence in the cab must have transformed it, so much so that the cabman, seeing me there with my head in the shadows of the roof and my knees against the window, had wondered perhaps if it was really his cab, really a cab. He hastens to look at his horse, and is reassured. But does one ever know oneself why one laughs? His laugh in any case was brief, which suggested I was not the joke. He closed the door and climbed back to his seat. It was not long then before the horse got under way.

Yes, surprising though it may seem, I still had a little money at this time. The small sum my father had left me as a gift, with no restrictions, at his death, I still wonder if it wasn't stolen from me. Then I had none. And yet my life went on, and even in the way I wanted, up to a point. The great disadvantage of this condition, which might be defined as the absolute impossibility of all purchase, is that it compels you to bestir yourself. It is rare, for example, when you are completely penniless, that you can have food brought to you from time to time in your retreat. You are therefore obliged to go out and bestir yourself, at least one day a week. You can hardly have a home address under these circumstances, it's inevitable. It was therefore with a certain delay that I learnt they were looking for me, for an affair concerning me. I forget through what channel. I did not read the newspapers, nor do I remember having spoken with anyone during these years, except perhaps three or four times, on the subject of food. At any rate, I must have had wind of the affair one way or another, otherwise I would never have gone to see the lawyer, Mr Nidder, strange how one fails to forget certain names, and he would never have received me. He verified my identity. That took some time. I showed him the metal initials in the lining of my hat, they proved nothing but they increased the probabilities. Sign, he said. He played with a cylindrical ruler, you could have felled an ox with it. Count, he said. A young woman, perhaps venal, was present at this interview, as a witness no doubt. I stuffed the wad in my pocket.

You shouldn't do that, he said. It occurred to me that he should have asked me to count before I signed, it would have been more in order. Where can I reach you, he said, if necessary? At the foot of the stairs I thought of something. Soon after I went back to ask him where this money came from, adding that I had a right to know. He gave me a woman's name that I've forgotten. Perhaps she had dandled me on her knees while I was still in swaddling clothes and there had been some lovey-dovey. Sometimes that suffices. I repeat, in swaddling clothes, for any later it would have been too late, for lovey-dovey. It is thanks to this money then that I still had a little. Very little. Divided by my life to come it was negligible, unless my conjectures were unduly pessimistic. I knocked on the partition beside my hat, right in the cabman's back if my calculations were correct. A cloud of dust rose from the upholstery. I took a stone from my pocket and knocked with the stone, until the cab stopped. I noticed that, unlike most vehicles, which slow down before stopping, the cab stopped dead. I waited. The whole cab shook. The cabman, on his high seat, must have been listening. I saw the horse as with my eyes of flesh. It had not lapsed into the drooping attitude of its briefest halts, it remained alert, its ears pricked up. I looked out of the window, we were again in motion. I banged again on the partition, until the cab stopped again. The cabman got down cursing from his seat. I lowered the window to prevent his opening the door. Faster, faster. He was redder than ever, purple in other words. Anger, or the rushing wind. I told him I was hiring him for the day. He replied that he had a funeral at three o'clock. Ah the dead. I told him I had changed my mind and no longer wished to go to the Zoo. Let us not go to the Zoo, I said. He replied that it made no difference to him where we went, provided it wasn't too far, because of his beast. And they talk to us about the specificity of primitive peoples' speech. I asked him if he knew of an eating-house. I added, You'll eat with me. I prefer being with a regular customer in such places. There was a long table with two benches of exactly the same length on either side. Across the table he spoke to me of his life, of his wife, of his beast, then again of his life, of the atrocious life that was his, chiefly because of his character. He asked me if I realized what it meant to be out of doors in all weathers. I learnt there were still some cabmen who spent their day snug and warm inside their cabs on the rank, waiting for a customer to come and rouse them. Such a thing was possible in the past, but nowadays other methods were necessary, if a man was to have a little laid up at the end of his days. I described my situation to him, what I had lost and what I was looking for. We did our best, both of us, to understand, to explain. He understood that I had lost my room and needed another, but all the rest escaped him. He had taken it into his head, whence nothing could ever dislodge it, that I was looking for a furnished room. He took from his pocket an evening paper of the day before, or perhaps the day before that again, and proceeded to run through the advertisements, five or six of which he underlined with a tiny pencil, the same that hovered over the likely outsiders. He underlined no doubt those he would have underlined if he had been in my shoes, or perhaps those concentrated in the same district, because of his beast. I would only have confused him by saying that I could tolerate no furniture in my room except the bed, and that all the other pieces, and even the very night table, had to be removed before I would consent to set foot in it. About three o'clock we roused the horse and set off again. The cabman suggested I climb up beside him on the seat, but for some time already I had been dreaming of the inside of the cab and I got back inside. We visited, methodically I hope, one after another, the addresses he had underlined. The short winter's day was drawing to a close. It seems to me sometimes that these are the only days I have ever known, and especially that most charming moment of all, just before night wipes them out. The addresses he had underlined, or rather marked with a cross, as common people do, proved fruitless one by one, and one by one he crossed them out with a diagonal stroke. Later he showed me the paper, advising me to keep it safe so as to be sure not to look again where I had already looked in vain. In spite of the closed windows, the creaking of the cab and the traffic noises, I heard him singing, all alone aloft on his high seat. He had preferred me to a funeral, this was a fact which would endure forever. He sang, *She is far from the land where her young hero,* those are the only words I remember. At each stop he got down from his seat and helped me get down from mine. I rang at the door he directed me to, and sometimes I disappeared inside the house. It was a strange feeling, I remember, a house all about me again, after so long. He waited for me on the sidewalk and helped me climb back into the cab. I was sick and tired of this cabman. He clambered back to his seat and we set off again. At a certain moment there occurred this. He stopped. I shook off my torpor and made ready to get down. But he did not come to open the door and offer me his arm, so that I was obliged to get down by myself. He was lighting the lamps. I love oil lamps, in spite of their having been, with candles, and if I except the stars, the first lights I ever knew. I asked him if I might light the second lamp, since he had already lit the first himself. He gave me his box of matches, I swung open on its hinges the little convex glass, lit and closed at once, so that the wick might burn steady and bright snug in its little house, sheltered from the wind. I had this joy. We saw nothing, by the light of these lamps, save the vague outlines of the horse, but the others saw them from afar, two yellow glows sailing slowly through the air. When the equipage turned an eye could be seen, red or green as the case might be, a bossy rhomb as clear and keen as stained glass.

After we had verified the last address the cabman suggested bringing me to a hotel he knew where I would be comfortable. That makes sense, cabman, hotel, it's plausible. With his recommendation I would want for nothing. Every convenience, he said, with a wink. I place this conversation on the sidewalk, in front of the house from which I had just emerged. I remember, beneath the lamp, the flank of the horse, hollow and damp, and on the handle of the door the cabman's hand in its woollen glove. The roof of the cab was on a level with my neck. I suggested we have a drink. The horse had neither eaten nor drunk all day. I mentioned this to the cabman, who replied that his beast would take no food till it was back in the stable. If it ate anything whatever, during work, were it but an apple or a lump of sugar, it would have stomach pains and colics that would root it to the spot and might even kill it. That was why he was compelled to tie its jaws together with a strap whenever for one reason or another he had to let it out of his sight, so that it would not have to suffer from the kind hearts of the passers-by. After a few drinks the cabman invited me to do his wife and him the honour of spending the night in their home. It was not far. Recollecting these emotions, with the celebrated advantage of tranquillity, it seems to me he did nothing else, all that day, but turn about his lodging. They lived above a stable, at the back of a yard. Ideal location, I could have done with it. Having presented me to his wife, extraordinarily full-bottomed, he left us. She was manifestly ill at ease, alone with me. I could understand her, I don't stand on ceremony on these occasions. No reason for this to end or go on. Then let it end. I said I would go down to the stable and sleep there. The cabman protested. I insisted. He drew his wife's attention to the pustule on top of my skull, for I had removed my hat out of civility. He should have that removed, she said. The cabman named a doctor he held in high esteem who had rid him of an induration of the seat. If he wants to sleep in the stable, said his wife, let him sleep in the stable. The cabman took the lamp from the table and preceded me down the stairs, or rather ladder, which descended to the stable, leaving his wife in the dark. He spread a horse blanket on the ground in a corner on the straw and left me a box of matches in case I needed to see clearly in the night. I don't remember what the horse was doing all this time. Stretched out in the dark I heard the noise it made as it drank, a noise like no other, the sudden gallop of the rats, and above me the muffled voices of the cabman and his wife as they criticized me. I held the box of matches in my hand, a big box of safety matches. I got up during the night and struck one. Its brief flame enabled me to locate the cab. I was seized, then abandoned, by the desire to set fire to the stable. I found the cab in the dark, opened the door, the rats poured out, I climbed in. As I settled down I noticed that the cab was no longer level, it was inevitable, with the shafts resting on the ground. It was better so, that allowed me to lie well back, with my feet higher than my head on the other seat. Several times during the night I felt the horse looking at me through the window and the breath of its nostrils. Now that it was unharnessed it must have been puzzled by my presence in the cab. I was cold, having forgotten to take the blanket, but not quite enough to go and get it. Through the window of the cab I saw the window of the stable, more and more clearly. I got out of the cab. It was not so dark now in the stable, I could make out the manger, the rack, the harness hanging, what else, buckets and brushes. I went to the door but couldn't open it. The horse didn't take its eyes off me. Don't horses ever sleep? It seemed to me the cabman should have tied it, to the manger for example. So I was obliged to leave by the window. It wasn't easy. But what is easy? I went out head first, my hands were flat on the ground of the yard while my legs were still thrashing to get clear of the frame. I remember the tufts of grass on which I pulled with both hands, in my efforts to extricate myself. I should have taken off my greatcoat and thrown it through the window, but that would have meant thinking of it. No sooner had I left the yard than I thought of something. Weakness. I slipped a banknote in the match box, went back to the yard and placed the box on the sill of the window through which I had just come. The horse was at the window. But after I had taken a few steps in the street I returned to the yard and took back my banknote. I left the matches, they were not mine. The horse was still at the window. I was sick and tired of this cabhorse. Dawn was just breaking. I did not know where I was. I made towards the rising sun, towards where I thought it should rise, the quicker to come into the light. I would have liked a sea horizon, or a desert one. When I am abroad in the morning, I go to meet the sun, and in the evening, when I am abroad, I follow it, till I am down among the dead. I don't know why I told this story. I could just as well have told another. Perhaps some other time I'll be able to tell another. Living souls, you will see how alike they are.

—Translated by RICHARD SEAVER
in collaboration with the author

THE CALMATIVE

I don't know when I died. It always seemed to me I died old, about ninety years old, and what years, and that my body bore it out, from head to foot. But this evening, alone in my icy bed, I have the feeling I'll be older than the day, the night, when the sky with all its lights fell upon me, the same I had so often gazed on since my first stumblings on the distant earth. For I'm too frightened this evening to listen to myself rot, waiting for the great red lapses of the heart, the tearings at the caecal walls, and for the slow killings to finish in my skull, the assaults on unshakable pillars, the fornications with corpses. So I'll tell myself a story, I'll try and tell myself another story, to try and calm myself, and it's there I feel I'll be old, old, even older than the day I fell, calling for help, and it came. Or is it possible that in this story I have come back to life, after my death? No, it's not like me to come back to life, after my death.

What possessed me to stir when I wasn't with anybody? Was I being thrown out? No, I wasn't with anybody. I see a kind of den littered with empty tins. And yet we are not in the country. Perhaps it's just ruins, a ruined folly, on the skirts of the town, in a field, for the fields come right up to our walls, their walls, and the cows lie down at night in the lee of the ramparts. I have changed refuge so often, in the course of my rout, that now I can't tell between dens and ruins. But there was never any city but the one. It is true you often move along in a dream, houses and factories darken the air, trams go by, and under your feet wet from the grass there are suddenly cobbles. I only know the city of my childhood, I must have seen the other, but unbelieving. All I say cancels out, I'll have said nothing. Was I hungry itself? Did the weather tempt me? It was cloudy and cool, I insist, but not to the extent of luring me out. I couldn't get up at the first attempt, nor let us say at the second, and once up, propped against the wall, I wondered if I could go on, I mean up, propped against the wall. Impossible to go out and walk. I speak as though it all happened yesterday. Yesterday indeed is recent, but not enough. For what I tell this evening is passing this evening, at this passing hour. I'm no longer with these assassins, in this bed of terror, but in my distant refuge, my hands twined together, my head bowed, weak, breathless, calm, free, and older than I'll have ever been, if my calculations are correct. I'll tell my story in the past none the less, as though it were a myth, or an old fable, for this evening I need another age, that age to become another age in which I became what I was.

But little by little I got myself out and started walking with short steps among the trees, oh look, trees! The paths of other days were rank with tangled growth. I leaned against the trunks to get my breath and pulled myself forward with the help of boughs. Of my last passage no trace remained. They were the perishing oaks immortalized by d'Aubigné. It was only a grove. The fringe was near, a light less green and kind of tattered told me so, in a whisper. Yes, no matter where you stood, in this little wood, and were it in the furthest recess of its poor secrecies, you saw on every hand the gleam of this pale light, promise of God knows what fatuous eternity. Die without too much pain, a little, that's worth your while. Under the blind sky close with your own hands the eyes soon sockets, then quick into carrion not to mislead the crows. That's the advantage of death by drowning, one of the advantages, the crabs never get there too soon. But here a strange thing, I was no sooner free of the wood at last, having crossed unminding the ditch that girdles it, than thoughts came to me of cruelty, the kind that smiles. A lush pasture lay before me, nonsuch perhaps, who cares, drenched in evening dew or recent rain. Beyond this meadow to my certain knowledge a path, then a field and finally the ramparts, closing the prospect. Cyclopean and crenellated, standing out faintly against a sky scarcely less sombre, they did not seem in ruins, viewed from mine, but were, to my certain knowledge. Such was the scene offered to me, in vain, for I knew it well and loathed it. What I saw was a bald man in a brown suit, a comedian. He was telling a funny story about a fiasco. Its point escaped me. He used the word snail, or slug, to the delight of all present. The women seemed even more entertained than their escorts, if that were possible. Their shrill laughter pierced the clapping and, when this had subsided, broke out still here and there in sudden peals even after the next story had begun, so that part of it was lost. Perhaps they had in mind the reigning penis sitting who knows by their side and from that sweet shore launched their cries of joy towards the comic vast, what a talent. But it's to me this evening something has to happen, to my body as in myth and metamorphosis, this old body to which nothing ever happened, or so little, which never met with anything, loved anything, wished for anything, in its tarnished universe, except for the mirrors to shatter, the plane, the curved, the magnifying, the minifying, and to vanish in the havoc of its images. Yes, this evening it has to be as in the story my father used to read to me, evening after evening, when I was small, and he had all his health, to calm me, evening after evening, year after year it seems to me this evening, which I don't remember much about, except that it was the adventures of one Joe Breem, or Breen, the son of a lighthouse-keeper, a strong muscular lad of fifteen, those were the words, who swam for miles in the night, a knife between his teeth, after a shark, I forget why, out of sheer heroism. He might have simply told me the story, he knew it by heart, so did I, but that wouldn't have calmed me, he had to read it to me, evening after evening, or pretend to read it to me, turning the pages and explaining the pictures that were of me already, evening after evening the same pictures, till I dozed off on his shoulder. If he had skipped a single word I would have hit him, with my little fist, in his big belly bursting out of the old cardigan and unbuttoned trousers that rested him from his office canonicals. For me now the setting forth, the struggle and perhaps the return, for the old man I am this evening, older than my father ever was, older than I shall ever be. I crossed the meadow with little stiff steps at the same time limp, the best I could manage. Of my last passage no trace remained, it was long ago. And the little bruised stems soon straighten up again, having need of air and light, and as for the broken their place is soon taken. I entered the town by what they call the Shepherds' Gate without having seen a soul, only the first bats like flying crucifixions, nor heard a sound except my steps, my heart in my breast and then, as I went under the arch, the hoot of an owl, that cry at once so soft and fierce which in the night, calling, answering, through my little wood and those nearby, sounded in my shelter like a tocsin. The further I went into the city the more I was struck by its deserted air. It was lit as usual, brighter than usual, although the shops were shut. But the lights were on in their windows with the object no doubt of attracting customers and prompting them to say, I say, I like that, not dear either, I'll come back tomorrow, if I'm still alive. I nearly said, Good God it's Sunday. The trams were running, the buses too, but few, slow, empty, noiseless, as if under water. I didn't see a single horse! I was wearing my long green greatcoat with the velvet collar, such as motorists wore about 1900, my father's, but that day it was sleeveless, a vast cloak. But on me it was still the same great dead weight, with no warmth to it, and the tails swept the ground, scraped it rather, they had grown so stiff, and I so shrunken. What would, what could happen to me in this empty place? But I felt the houses packed with people, lurking behind the curtains they looked out into the street or, crouched far back in the depths of the room, head in hands, were sunk in dream. Up aloft my hat, the same as always, I reached no further. I went right across the city and came to the sea, having followed the river to its mouth. I kept saying, I'll go back, unbelieving. The boats at anchor in the harbour, tied up to the jetty, seemed no less numerous than usual, as if I knew anything about what was usual. But the quays were deserted and there was no sign or stir of arrival or departure. But all might change from one moment to the next and be transformed like magic before my eyes. Then all the bustle of the people and things of the sea, the masts of the big craft gravely rocking and of the small more jauntily, I insist, and I'd hear the gulls' terrible cry and perhaps the sailors' cry. And I might slip unnoticed aboard a freighter outward bound and get far away and spend far away a few good months, perhaps even a year or two, in the sun, in peace, before I died. And without going that far it would be a sad state of affairs if in that unscandalizable throng I couldn't achieve a little encounter that would calm me a little, or exchange a few words with a navigator for example, words to carry away with me to my refuge, to add to my collection. I waited sitting on a kind of topless capstan, saying, The very capstans this evening are out of order. And I gazed out to sea, out beyond the breakwaters, without sighting the least vessel. I could see lights flush with the water. And the pretty beacons at the harbour mouth I could see too, and others in the distance, flashing from the coast, the islands, the headlands. But seeing still no sign or stir I made ready to go, to turn away sadly from this dead haven, for there are scenes that call for strange farewells. I had merely to bow my head and look down at my feet, for it is in this attitude I always drew the strength to, how shall I say, I don't know, and it was always from the earth, rather than from the sky, notwithstanding its reputation, that my help came in time of trouble. And there, on the flagstone, which I was not focussing, for why focus it, I saw haven afar, where the black swell was most perilous, and all about me storm and wreck. I'll never come back here, I said. But when with a thrust of both hands against the rim of the capstan I heaved myself up I found facing me a young boy holding a goat by a horn. I sat down again. He stood there silent looking at me without visible fear or revulsion. Admittedly the light was poor. His silence seemed natural to me, it befitted me as the elder to speak first. He was barefoot and in rags. Haunter of the waterfront he had stepped aside to see what the dark hulk could be abandoned on the quayside. Such was my train of thought. Close up to me now with his little guttersnipe's eye there could be no doubt left in his mind. And yet he stayed. Can this base thought be mine? Moved, for after all that is what I must have come out for, in a way, and with little expectation of advantage from what might follow, I resolved to speak to him. So I marshalled the words and opened my mouth, thinking I would hear them. But all I heard was a kind of rattle, unintelligible even to me who knew what was intended. But it was nothing, mere speechlessness due to long silence, as in the wood that darkens the mouth of hell, do you remember, I only just. Without letting go of his goat he moved right up against me and offered me a sweet out of a twist of paper such as you could buy for a penny. I hadn't been offered a sweet for eighty years at least, but I took it eagerly and put it in my mouth, the old gesture came back to me, more and more moved since that is what I wanted. The sweets were stuck together and I had my work cut out to separate the top one, a green one, from the others, but he helped me and his hand brushed mine. And a moment later as he made to move away, hauling his goat after him, with a great gesticulation of my whole body I motioned him to stay and I said, in an impetuous murmur, Where are you off to, my little man, with your nanny? The words were hardly out of my mouth when for shame I covered my face. And yet they were the same I had tried to utter but a moment before. Where are you off to, my little man, with your nanny! If I could have blushed I would have, but there was not enough blood left in my extremities. If I had had a penny in my pocket I would have given it to him, for him to forgive me, but I did not have a penny in my pocket, nor anything resembling it. Nothing that could give pleasure to a little unfortunate at the mouth of life. I suspect I had nothing with me but my stone, that day, having gone out as it were without premeditation. Of his little person I was fated to see no more than the black curly hair and the pretty curve of the long bare legs all muscle and dirt. And the hand, so fresh and keen, I would not forget in a hurry either. I looked for better words to say to him, I found them too late, he was gone, oh not far, but far. Out of my life too he went without a care, not one of his thoughts would ever be for me again, unless perhaps when he was old and, delving in his boyhood, would come upon that gallows night and hold the goat by the horn again and linger again a moment by my side, with who knows perhaps a touch of tenderness, even of envy, but I have my doubts. Poor dear dumb beasts, how you will have helped me. What does your daddy do? that's what I would have said to him if he had given me the chance. Soon they were no more than a single blur which if I hadn't known I might have taken for a young centaur. I was nearly going to have the goat dung, then pick up a handful of the pellets so soon cold and hard, sniff and even taste them, no, that would not help me this evening. I say this evening as if it were always the same evening, but are there two evenings? I went, intending to get back as fast as I could, but it would not be quite empty-handed, repeating, I'll never come back here. My legs were paining me, every step would gladly have been the last, but the glances I darted towards the windows, stealthily, showed me a great cylinder sweeping past as though on rollers on the asphalt. I must indeed have been moving fast, for I overhauled more than one pedestrian, there are the first men, without extending myself, I who in the normal way was left standing by cripples, and then I seemed to hear the footfalls die behind me. And yet each little step would gladly have been the last. So much so that when I emerged on a square I hadn't noticed on the way out, with a cathedral looming on the far side, I decided to go in, if it was open, and hide, as in the Middle Ages, for a space. I say cathedral, it may not have been, I don't know, all I know is it would vex me in this story that aspires to be the last, to have taken refuge in a common church. I remarked the Saxon Stützenwechsel. Charming effect, but it didn't charm me. The brilliantly lit nave appeared deserted. I walked round it several times without seeing a soul. They were hiding perhaps, under the choir-stalls, or dodging behind the pillars, like woodpeckers. Suddenly close to where I was, and without my having heard the long preliminary rumblings, the organ began to boom. I sprang up from the mat on which I lay before the altar and hastened to the far end of the nave as if on my way out. But it was a side aisle and the door I disappeared through was not the exit. For instead of being restored to the night I found myself at the foot of a spiral staircase which I began to climb at top speed, mindless of my heart, like one hotly pursued by a homicidal maniac. This staircase faintly lit by I know not what means, slits perhaps, I mounted panting as far as the projecting gallery in which it culminated and which, separated from the void by a cynical parapet, encompassed a smooth round wall capped by a little dome covered with lead or verdigrised copper, phew, if that's not clear. People must have come here for the view, those who fall die on the way. Flattening myself against the wall I started round, clockwise. But I had hardly gone a few steps when I met a man revolving in the other direction, with the utmost circumspection. How I'd love to push him, or him to push me, over the edge. He gazed at me wild-eyed for a moment and then, not daring to pass me on the parapet side and surmising correctly that I would not relinquish the wall just to oblige him, abruptly turned his back on me, his head rather, for his back remained glued to the wall, and went back the way he had come so that soon there was nothing left of him but a left hand. It lingered a moment, then slid out of sight. All that remained to me was the vision of two burning eyes starting out of their sockets under a check cap. Into what nightmare thingness am I fallen? My hat flew off, but did not get far thanks to the string. I turned my head towards the staircase and lent an eye. Nothing. Then a little girl came into view followed by a man holding her by the hand, both pressed against the wall. He pushed her into the stairway, disappeared after her, turned and raised towards me a face that made me recoil. I could only see his bare head above the top step. When they were gone I called. I completed in haste the round of the gallery. No one. I saw on the horizon, where sky, sea, plain and mountain meet, a few low stars, not to be confused with the fires men light, at night, or that go alight alone. Enough. Back in the street I tried to find my way in the sky, where I knew the Bears so well. If I had seen someone I would have stopped him to ask, the most ferocious aspect would not have daunted me. I would have said, touching my hat, Pardon me your honour, the Shepherds' Gate for the love of God. I thought I could go no further, but no sooner had the impetus reached my legs than on I went, believe it or not, at a very fair pace. I wasn't returning empty-handed, not quite, I was taking back with me the virtual certainty that I was still of this world, of that world too, in a way. But I was paying the price. I would have done better to spend the night in the cathedral, on the mat before the altar, I would have continued on my way at first light, or they would have found me stretched out in the rigor of death, the genuine bodily article, under the blue eyes fount of so much hope, and put me in the evening papers. But suddenly I was descending a wide street, vaguely familiar, but in which I could never have set foot, in my lifetime. But soon realizing I was going downhill I turned about and set off in the other direction. For I was afraid if I went downhill of returning to the sea where I had sworn never to return. When I say I turned about I mean I wheeled round in a wide semi-circle without slowing down, for I was afraid if I stopped of not being able to start again, yes, I was afraid of that too. And this evening too I dare not stop. I was struck more and more by the contrast between the brightly lit streets and their deserted air. To say it distressed me, no, but I say it all the same, in the hope of calming myself. To say there was no one abroad, no, I would not go that far, for I remarked a number of shapes, male and female, strange shapes, but not more so than usual. As to what hour it might have been I had no idea, except that it must have been some hour of the night. But it might have been three or four in the morning just as it might have been ten or eleven in the evening, depending no doubt on whether one wondered at the scarcity of passers-by or at the extraordinary radiance shed by the street-lamps and traffic-lights. For at one or other of these no one could fail to wonder, unless he was out of his mind. Not a single private car, but admittedly from time to time a public vehicle, slow sweep of light silent and empty. It is not my wish to labour these antinomies, for we are needless to say in a skull, but I have no choice but to add the following few remarks. All the mortals I saw were alone and as if sunk in themselves. It must be a common sight, but mixed with something else I imagine. The only couple was two men grappling, their legs intertwined. I only saw one cyclist! He was going the same way as I was. All were going the same way as I was, vehicles too, I have only just realized it. He was pedalling slowly in the middle of the street, reading a newspaper which he held with both hands spread open before his eyes. Every now and then he rang his bell without interrupting his reading. I watched him recede till he was no more than a dot on the horizon. Suddenly a young woman perhaps of easy virtue, dishevelled and her dress in disarray, darted across the street like a rabbit. That is all I had to add. But here a strange thing, yet another, I had no pain whatever, not even in my legs. Weakness. A good night's nightmare and a tin of sardines would restore my sensitivity. My shadow, one of my shadows, flew before me, dwindled, slid under my feet, trailed behind me the way shadows will. This degree of opacity appeared to me conclusive. But suddenly ahead of me a man on the same side of the street and going the same way, to keep harping on the same thing lest I forget. The distance between us was considerable, seventy paces at least, and fearing he might escape me I quickened my step with the result I swept forward as if on rollers. This is not me, I said, let us make the most of it. Finding myself in an instant a bare ten paces in his rear I slowed down so as not to burst in on him and so heighten the aversion my person inspired even in its most abject and obsequious attitudes. And a moment later, keeping humbly in step with him, Excuse me your honour, the Shepherds' Gate for the love of God! At close quarters he appeared normal apart from that air already noted of ebbing inward. I drew a few steps ahead, turned, cringed, touched my hat and said, The right time for mercy's sake! I might as well not have existed. But what about the sweet? A light! I cried. Given my need of help I can't think why I did not bar his path. I couldn't have, that's all, I couldn't have touched him. Seeing a stone seat by the kerb I sat down and crossed my legs, like Walther. I must have dozed off, for the next thing was a man sitting beside me. I was still taking him in when he opened his eyes and set them on me, as if for the first time, for he shrank back unaffectedly. Where did you spring from?

he said. To hear myself addressed again so soon impressed me greatly. What's the matter with you? he said. I tried to look like one with whom that only is the matter which is native to him. Forgive me your honour, I said, gingerly lifting my hat and rising a fraction from the seat, the right time for the love of God! He said a time, I don't remember which, a time that explained nothing, that's all I remember, and did not calm me. But what time could have done that? Oh I know, I know, one will come that will. But in the meantime? What's that you said? he said. Unfortunately I had said nothing. But I wriggled out of it by asking him if he could help me find my way which I had lost. No, he said, for I am not from these parts and if I am sitting on this slab it is because the hotels were full or would not let me in, I have no opinion. But tell me the story of your life, then we'll see. My life! I cried. Why yes, he said, you know, that kind of— what shall I say? He brooded for a time, no doubt trying to think of what life could well be said to be a kind. In the end he went on, testily, Come now, everyone knows that. He jogged me in the ribs. No details, he said, the main drift, the main drift. But as I remained silent he said, Shall I tell you mine, then you'll see what I mean. The account he then gave was brief and dense, facts, without comment. That's what I call a life, he said, do you follow me now? It wasn't bad, his story, positively fairy-like in places. But that Pauline, I said, are you still with her? I am, he said, but I'm going to leave her and set up with another, younger and plumper. You travel a lot, I said. Oh widely, widely, he said. Words were coming back to me, and the way to make them sound. All that's a thing of the past for you no doubt, he said. Do you think of spending some time among us? I said. This sentence struck me as particularly well turned. If it's not a rude question, he said, how old are you? I don't know, I said. You don't know! he cried. Not exactly, I said. Are thighs much in your thoughts, he said, arses, cunts and environs. I didn't follow. No more erections naturally, he said. Erections? I said. The penis, he said, you know what the penis is, there, between the legs. Ah that, I said. It thickens, lengthens, stiffens and rises, he said, does it not? I assented, though they were not the terms I would have used. That is what we call an erection, he said. He pondered, then exclaimed, Phenomenal! No? Strange right enough, I said. And there you have it all, he said. But what will become of her? I said. Who? he said. Pauline, I said. She will grow old, he said with tranquil assurance, slowly at first, then faster and faster, in pain and bitterness, pulling the devil by the tail. The face was not full, but I eyed it in vain, it remained clothed in its flesh instead of turning all chalky and channelled as with a gouge. The very vomer kept its cushion. It is true discussion was always bad for me. I longed for the tender nonsuch, I would have trodden it gently, with my boots in my hand, and for the shade of my wood, far from this terrible light. What are you grinning and bearing? he said. He held on his knees a big black bag, like a midwife's I imagine. It was full of glittering phials. I asked him if they were all alike. Oho no, he said, for every taste. He took one and held it out to me, saying, One and six. What did he want? To sell it to me? Proceeding on this hypothesis I told him I had no money. No money! he cried. All of a sudden his hand came down on the back of my neck, his sinewy fingers closed and with a jerk and a twist he had me up against him. But instead of dispatching me he began to murmur words so sweet that I went limp and my head fell forward in his lap. Between the caressing voice and the fingers rowelling my neck the contrast was striking. But gradually the two things merged in a devastating hope, if I dare say so, and I dare. For this evening I have nothing to lose that I can discern. And if I have reached this point (in my story) without anything having changed, for if anything had changed I think I'd know, the fact remains I have reached it, and that's something, and with nothing changed, and that's something too. It's no excuse for rushing matters. No, it must cease gently, as gently cease on the stairs the steps of the loved one, who could not love and will not come back, and whose steps say so, that she could not love and will not come back. He suddenly shoved me away and showed me the phial again. There you have it all, he said. It can't have been the same all as before. Want it? he said. No, but I said yes, so as not to vex him. He proposed an exchange. Give me your hat, he said. I refused. What vehemence! he said. I haven't a thing, I said. Try in your pockets, he said. I haven't a thing, I said, I came out without a thing. Give me a lace, he said. I refused. Long silence. And if you gave me a kiss, he said finally. I knew there were kisses in the air. Can you take off your hat? he said. I took it off. Put it back, he said, you look nicer with it on. I put it on. Come on, he said, give me a kiss and let there be an end to it. Did it not occur to him I might turn him down? No, a kiss is not a bootlace, he must have seen from my face that all passion was not quite spent. Come, he said. I wiped my mouth in its tod of hair and advanced it towards his. Just a moment, he said. My mouth stood still. You know what a kiss is? he said. Yes yes, I said? If it's not a rude question, he said, when was your last? Some time ago, I said, but I can still do them. He took off his hat, a bowler, and tapped the middle of his forehead. There, he said, and there only. He had a noble brow, white and high. He leaned forward, closing his eyes. Quick, he said? I pursed up my lips as mother had taught me and brought them down where he had said. Enough, he said. He raised his hand towards the spot, but left the gesture unfinished and put on his hat. I turned away and looked across the street. It was then I noticed we were sitting opposite a horse-butcher's. Here, he said, take it. I had forgotten. He rose. Standing he was quite short. One good turn, he said, with radiant smile. His teeth shone. I listened to his steps die away. How tell what remains. But it's the end. Or have I been dreaming, am I dreaming? No no, none of that, for dream is nothing, a joke, and significant what is worse. I said, Stay where you are till day breaks, wait sleeping till the lamps go out and the streets come to life. But I stood up and moved off. My pains were back, but with something untoward which prevented my wrapping them round me. But I said, Little by little you are coming to. From my gait alone, slow, stiff and which seemed at every step to solve a statodynamic problem never posed before, I would have been known again, if I had been known. I crossed over and stopped before the butcher's. Behind the grille the curtains were drawn, rough canvas curtains striped blue and white, colours of the Virgin, and stained with great pink stains. They did not quite meet in the middle, and through the chink I could make out the dim carcasses of the gutted horses hanging from hooks head downwards. I hugged the walls, famished for shadow. To think that in a moment all will be said, all to do again. And the city clocks, what was wrong with them, whose great chill clang even in my wood fell on me from the air? What else? Ah yes, my spoils. I tried to think of Pauline, but she eluded me, gleamed an instant and was gone, like the young woman in the street. So I went in the atrocious brightness, buried in my old flesh, straining towards an issue and passing them by to left and right, and my mind panting after this and that and always flung back to where there was nothing. I succeeded however in fastening briefly on the little girl, long enough to see her a little more clearly than before, so that she wore a kind of bonnet and clasped in her hand a book, of common prayer perhaps, and to try and have her smile, but she did not smile, but vanished down the staircase without having yielded me her little face. I had to stop. At first nothing, then little by little, I mean rising up out of the silence till suddenly no higher, a kind of massive murmur coming perhaps from the house that was propping me up. That reminded me that the houses were full of people, besieged, no, I don't know. When I stepped back to look at the windows I could see, in spite of shutters, blinds and muslins, that many of the rooms were lit. The light was so dimmed by the brilliancy flooding the boulevard that short of knowing or suspecting it was not so one might have supposed everyone sleeping. The sound was not continuous, but broken by silences possibly of consternation. I thought of ringing at the door and asking for shelter and protection till morning. But suddenly I was on my way again. But little by little, in a slow swoon, darkness fell about me. I saw a mass of bright flowers fade in an exquisite cascade of paling colours. I found myself admiring, all along the housefronts, the gradual blossoming of squares and rectangles, casement and sash, yellow, green, pink, according to the curtains and blinds, finding that pretty. Then at last, before I fell, first to my knees, as cattle do, then on my face, I was in a throng. I didn't lose consciousness, when I lose consciousness it will not be to recover it. They paid no heed to me, though careful not to walk on me, a courtesy that must have touched me, it was what I had come out for. It was well with me, sated with dark and calm, lying at the feet of mortals, fathom deep in the grey of dawn, if it was dawn. But reality, too tired to look for the right word, was soon restored, the throng fell away, the light came back and I had no need to raise my head from the ground to know I was back in the same blinding void as before. I said, Stay where you are, down on the friendly stone, or at least indifferent, don't open your eyes, wait for morning. But up with me again and back on the way that was not mine, on uphill along the boulevard. A blessing he was not waiting for me, poor old Breem, or Breen. I said, The sea is east, it's west I must go, to the left of north. But in vain I raised without hope my eyes to the sky to look for the Bears. For the light I steeped in put out the stars, assuming they were there, which I doubted, remembering the clouds.

—Translated by the author

THE END

They clothed me and gave me money. I knew what the money was for, it was to get me started. When it was gone I would have to get more, if I wanted to go on. The same for the shoes, when they were worn out I would have to get them mended, or get myself another pair, or go on barefoot, if I wanted to go on. The same for the coat and trousers, needless to say, with this difference, that I could go on in my shirtsleeves, if I wanted. The clothes—shoes, socks, trousers, shirt, coat, hat—were not new, but the deceased must have been about my size. That is to say, he must have been a little shorter, a little thinner, for the clothes did not fit me so well in the beginning as they did at the end, the shirt especially, and it was many a long day before I could button it at the neck, or profit by the collar that went with it, or pin the skirts together between my legs in the way my mother had taught me. He must have put on his Sunday best to go to the consultation, perhaps for the first time, unable to bear it any longer. Be that as it may the hat was a bowler, in good shape. I said, Keep your hat and give me back mine. I added, Give me back my greatcoat. They replied that they had burnt them, together with my other clothes. I understood then that the end was near, at least fairly near. Later on I tried to exchange this hat for a cap, or a slouch which could be pulled down over my face, but without much success. And yet I could not go about bare-headed, with my skull in the state it was. At first this hat was too small, then it got used to me. They gave me a tie, after long discussion. It seemed a pretty tie to me, but I didn't like it. When it came at last I was too tired to send it back. But in the end it came in useful. It was blue, with kinds of little stars. I didn't feel well, but they told me I was well enough. They didn't say in so many words that I was as well as I would ever be, but that was the implication. I lay inert on the bed and it took three women to put on my trousers. They didn't seem to take much interest in my private parts which to tell the truth were nothing to write home about, I didn't take much interest in them myself. But they might have passed some remark. When they had finished I got up and finished dressing unaided. They told me to sit on the bed and wait. All the bedding had disappeared. It made me angry that they had not let me wait in the familiar bed, instead of leaving me standing in the cold, in these clothes that smelt of sulphur. I said, You might have left me in bed till the last moment. Men all in white came in with mallets in their hands. They dismantled the bed and took away the pieces. One of the women followed them out and came back with a chair which she set before me. I had done well to pretend I was angry. But to make it quite clear to them how angry I was that they had not left me in my bed, I gave the chair a kick that sent it flying. A man came in and made a sign to me to follow him. In the hall he gave me a paper to sign. What's this, I said, a safe-conduct? It's a receipt, he said, for the

clothes and money you have received. What money? I said. It was then I received the money. To think I had almost departed without a penny in my pocket. The sum was not large, compared to other sums, but to me it seemed large. I saw the familiar objects, companions of so many bearable hours. The stool, for example, dearest of all. The long afternoons together, waiting for it to be time for bed. At times I felt its wooden life invade me, till I myself became a piece of old wood. There was even a hole for my cyst. Then the window pane with the patch of frosting gone, where I used to press my eye in the hour of need, and rarely in vain. I am greatly obliged to you, I said, is there a law which prevents you from throwing me out naked and penniless? That would damage our reputation in the long run, he replied. Could they not possibly keep me a little longer, I said, I could make myself useful. Useful, he said, joking apart you would be willing to make yourself useful? A moment later he went on, If they believed you were really willing to make yourself useful they would keep you, I am sure. The number of times I had said I was going to make myself useful, I wasn't going to start that again. How weak I felt! Perhaps, I said, they would consent to take back the money and keep me a little longer. This is a charitable institution, he said, and the money is a gift you receive when you leave. When it is gone you will have to get more, if you wish to go on. Never come back here whatever you do, you would not be let in. Don't go to any of our branches either, they would turn you away. Exelmans! I cried. Come come, he said, and anyway no one understands a tenth of what you say. I'm so old, I said. You are not so old as all that, he said. May I stay here just a little longer, I said, till the rain is over. You may wait in the cloister, he said, the rain will go on all day. You may wait in the cloister till six o'clock, you will hear the bell. If anyone challenges you, you need only say you have permission to shelter in the cloister. Whose name will I give? I said. Weir, he said.

I had not been long in the cloister when the rain stopped and the sun came out. It was low and I reckoned it must be getting on for six, considering the season. I stayed there looking through the archway at the sun as it went down behind the cloister. A man appeared and asked me what I was doing. What do you want? were the words he used. Very friendly. I replied that I had Mr Weir's permission to stay in the cloister till six o'clock. He went away, but came back immediately. He must have spoken to Mr Weir in the interim, for he said, You must not loiter in the cloister now the rain is over.

Now I was making my way through the garden. There was that strange light which follows a day of persistent rain, when the sun comes out and the sky clears too late to be of any use. The earth makes a sound as of sighs and the last drops fall from the emptied, cloudless sky. A small boy, stretching out his hands and looking up at the blue sky, asked his mother how such a thing was possible. Fuck off, she said. I suddenly remembered I had not thought of asking Mr Weir for a piece of bread. He would surely have given it to me. I had as a matter of fact thought of it during our conversation in the hall. I had said to myself, Let us first finish our conversation, then I'll ask. I knew well they would not keep me. I would gladly have turned back, but I was afraid one of the guards would stop me and tell me I would never see Mr Weir again. That might have added to my sorrow. And anyway I never turned back on such occasions.

In the street I was lost. I had not set foot in this part of the city for a long time and it seemed greatly changed. Whole buildings had disappeared, the palings had changed position, and on all sides I saw, in great letters, the names of tradesmen I had never seen before and would have been at a loss to pronounce. There were streets where I remembered none, some I did remember had vanished and others had completely changed their names. The general impression was the same as before. It is true I did not know the city very well. Perhaps it was quite a different one. I did not know where I was supposed to be going. I had the great good fortune, more than once, not to be run over. My appearance still made people laugh, with that hearty jovial laugh so good for the health. By keeping the red part of the sky as much as possible on my right hand I came at last to the river. Here all seemed at first sight more or less as I had left it. But if I had looked more closely I would doubtless have discovered many changes. And indeed I subsequently did so. But the general appearance of the river, flowing between its quays and under its bridges, had not changed. Yes, the river still gave the impression it was flowing in the wrong direction. That's all a pack of lies I feel. My bench was still there. It was shaped to fit the curves of the seated body. It stood beside a watering trough, gift of a Mrs Maxwell to the city horses, according to the inscription. During the short time I rested there several horses took advantage of this monument. The iron shoes approached and the jingle of the harness. Then silence. That was the horse looking at me. Then the noise of pebbles and mud that horses make when drinking. Then the silence again. That was the horse looking at me again. Then the pebbles again. Then the silence again. Till the horse had finished drinking or the driver deemed it had drunk its fill. The horses were uneasy. Once, when the noise stopped, I turned and saw the horse looking at me. The driver too was looking at me. Mrs Maxwell would have been pleased if she could have seen her trough rendering such services to the city horses. When it was night, after a tedious twilight, I took off my hat which was paining me. I longed to be under cover again, in an empty place, close and warm, with artificial light, an oil lamp for choice, with a pink shade for preference. From time to time someone would come to make sure I was all right and needed nothing. It was long since I had longed for anything and the effect on me was horrible.

In the days that followed I visited several lodgings, without much success. They usually slammed the door in my face, even when I showed my money and offered to pay a week in advance, or even two. It was in vain I put on my best manners, smiled and spoke distinctly, they slammed the door in my face before I could even finish my little speech. It was at this time I perfected a method of doffing my hat at once courteous and discreet, neither servile nor insolent. I slipped it smartly forward, held it a second poised in such a way that the person addressed could not see my skull, then slipped it back. To do that naturally, without creating an unfavorable impression, is no easy matter. When I deemed that to tip my hat would suffice, I naturally did no more than tip it. But to tip one's hat is no easy matter either. I subsequently solved this problem, always fundamental in time of adversity, by wearing a kepi and saluting in military fashion, no, that must be wrong, I don't know, I had my hat at the end. I never made the mistake of wearing medals. Some landladies were in such need of money that they let me in immediately and showed me the room. But I couldn't come to an agreement with any of them. Finally I found a basement. With this woman I came to an agreement at once. My oddities, that's the expression she used, did not alarm her. She nevertheless insisted on making the bed and cleaning the room once a week, instead of once a month as I requested. She told me that while she was cleaning, which would not take long, I could wait in the area. She added, with a great deal of feeling, that she would never put me out in bad weather. This woman was Greek, I think, or Turkish. She never spoke about herself. I somehow got the idea she was a widow or at least that her husband had left her. She had a strange accent. But so had I with my way of assimilating the vowels and omitting the consonants.

Now I didn't know where I was. I had a vague vision, not a real vision, I didn't see anything, of a big house five or six stories high, one of a block perhaps. It was dusk when I got there and I did not pay the same heed to my surroundings as I might have done if I had suspected they were to close about me. And by then I must have lost all hope. It is true that when I left this house it was a glorious day, but I never look back when leaving. I must have read somewhere, when I was small and still read, that it is better not to look back when leaving. And yet I sometimes did. But even without looking back it seems to me I should have seen something when leaving. But there it is. All I remember is my feet emerging from my shadow, one after the other. My shoes had stiffened and the sun brought out the cracks in the leather.

I was comfortable enough in this house, I must say. Apart from a few rats I was alone in the basement. The woman did her best to respect our agreement. About noon she brought me a big tray of food and took away the tray of the previous day. At the same time she brought me a clean chamber-pot. The chamber-pot had a large handle which she slipped over her arm, so that both her hands were free to carry the tray. The rest of the day I saw no more of her except sometimes when she peeped in to make sure nothing had happened to me. Fortunately I did not need affection. From my bed I saw the feet coming and going on the sidewalk. Certain evenings, when the weather was fine and I felt equal to it, I fetched my chair into the area and sat looking up into the skirts of the women passing by. Once I sent for a crocus bulb and planted it in the dark area, in an old pot. It must have been coming up to spring, it was probably not the right time for it. I left the pot outside, attached to a string I passed through the window. In the evening, when the weather was fine, a little light crept up the wall. Then I sat down beside the window and pulled on the string to keep the pot in the light and warmth. That can't have been easy, I don't see how I managed it. It was probably not the right thing for it. I manured it as best I could and pissed on it when the weather was dry. It may not have been the right thing for it.

It sprouted, but never any flowers, just a wilting stem and a few chlorotic leaves. I would have liked to have a yellow crocus, or a hyacinth, but there, it was not to be. She wanted to take it away, but I told her to leave it. She wanted to buy me another, but I told her I didn't want another. What lacerated me most was the din of the newspaper boys. They went pounding by every day at the same hours, their heels thudding on the sidewalk, crying the names of their papers and even the headlines. The house noises disturbed me less. A little girl, unless it was a little boy, sang every evening at the same hour, somewhere above me. For a long time I could not catch the words. But hearing them day after day I finally managed to catch a few. Strange words for a little girl, or a little boy. Was it a song in my head or did it merely come from without? It was a sort of lullaby, I believe. It often sent me to sleep, even me. Sometimes it was a little girl who came. She had long red hair hanging down in two braids. I didn't know who she was. She lingered awhile in the room, then went away without a word. One day I had a visit from a policeman. He said I had to be watched, without explaining why. Suspicious, that was it, he told me I was suspicious. I let him talk. He didn't dare arrest me. Or perhaps he had a kind heart. A priest too, one day I had a visit from a priest. I informed him I belonged to a branch of the reformed church. He asked me what kind of clergyman I would like to see. Yes, there's that about the reformed church, you're lost, it's unavoidable. Perhaps he had a kind heart. He told me to let him know if I ever needed a helping hand. A helping hand! He gave me his name and explained where I could reach him. I should have made a note of it.

One day the woman made me an offer. She said she was in urgent need of cash and that if I could pay her six months in advance she would reduce my rent by one fourth during that period, something of that kind. This had the advantage of saving six weeks' (?) rent and the disadvantage of almost exhausting my small capital. But could you call that a disadvantage? Wouldn't I stay on in any case till my last penny was gone, and even longer, till she put me out? I gave her the money and she gave me a receipt.

One morning, not long after this transaction, I was awakened by a man shaking my shoulder. It could not have been much past eleven. He requested me to get up and leave his house immediately. He was most correct, I must say. His surprise, he said, was no less than mine. It was his house. His property. The Turkish woman had left the day before. But I saw her last night, I said. You must be mistaken, he said, for she brought the keys to my office no later than yesterday afternoon. But I just paid her six months' rent in advance, I said. Get a refund, he said. But I don't even know her name, I said, let alone her address. You don't know her name? he said. He must have thought I was lying. I'm sick, I said, I can't leave like this, without any notice. You're not so sick as all that, he said. He offered to send for a taxi, even an ambulance if I preferred. He said he needed the room immediately for his pig which even as he spoke was catching cold in a cart before the door and no one to look after him but a stray urchin whom he had never set eyes on before and who was probably busy tormenting him.

I asked if he couldn't let me have another place, any old corner where I could lie down long enough to recover from the shock and decide what to do. He said he could not. Don't think I'm being unkind, he added. I could live here with the pig, I said, I'd look after him. The long months of peace, wiped out in an instant! Come now, come now, he said, get a grip on yourself, be a man, get up, that's enough. After all it was no concern of his. He had really been most patient. He must have visited the basement while I was sleeping.

I felt weak. Perhaps I was. I stumbled in the blinding light. A bus took me into the country. I sat down in a field in the sun. But it seems to me that was much later. I stuck leaves under my hat, all the way round, to make a shade. The night was cold. I wandered for hours in the fields. At last I found a heap of dung. The next day I started back to the city. They made me get off three buses. I sat down by the roadside and dried my clothes in the sun. I enjoyed doing that. I said to myself, There's nothing more to be done now, not a thing, till they are dry. When they were dry I brushed them with a brush, I think a kind of curry-comb, that I found in a stable. Stables have always been my salvation. Then I went to the house and begged a glass of milk and a slice of bread and butter. They gave me everything except the butter. May I rest in the stable? I said. No, they said. I still stank, but with a stink that pleased me. I much preferred it to my own which moreover it prevented me from smelling, except a waft now and then. In the days that followed I took the necessary steps to recover my money. I don't know exactly what happened, whether I couldn't find the address, or whether there was no such address, or whether the Greek woman was unknown there. I ransacked my pockets for the receipt, to try and decipher the name. It wasn't there. Perhaps she had taken it back while I was sleeping. I don't know how long I wandered thus, resting now in one place, now in another, in the city and in the country. The city had suffered many changes. Nor was the country as I remembered it. The general effect was the same. One day I caught sight of my son. He was striding along with a briefcase under his arm. He took off his hat and bowed and I saw he was as bald as a coot. I was almost certain it was he. I turned round to gaze after him. He went bustling along on his duck feet, bowing and scraping and flourishing his hat left and right. The insufferable son of a bitch.

One day I met a man I had known in former times. He lived in a cave by the sea. He had an ass that grazed winter and summer, over the cliffs, or along the little tracks leading down to the sea. When the weather was very bad this ass came down to the cave of his own accord and sheltered there till the storm was past. So they had spent many a night huddled together, while the wind howled and the sea pounded on the shore. With the help of this ass he could deliver sand, seawrack, and shells to the townsfolk, for their gardens. He couldn't carry much at a time, for the ass was old and small and the town was far. But in this way he earned a little money, enough to keep him in tobacco and matches and to buy a piece of bread from time to time. It was during one of these excursions that he met me, in the suburbs. He was delighted to see me, poor man. He begged me to go home with him and spend the night. Stay as long as you like, he said. What's

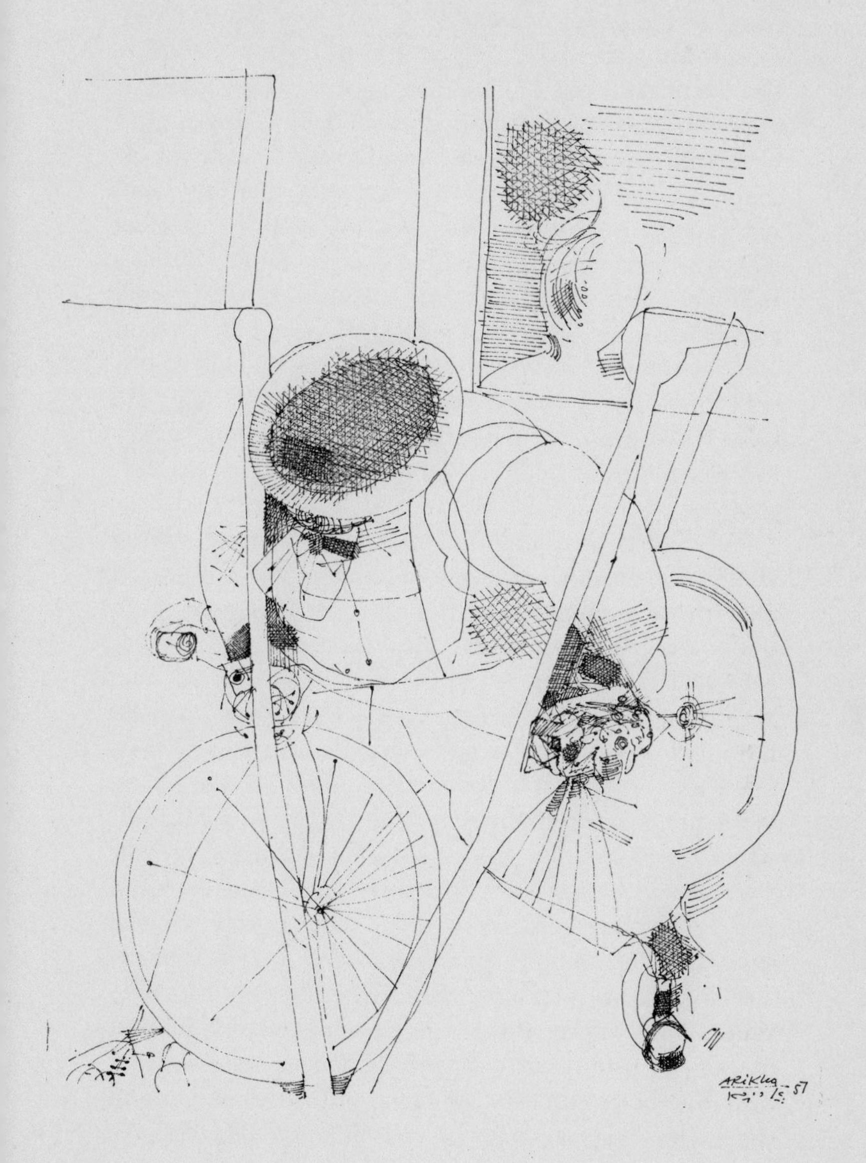
ARiKha 57

wrong with your ass? I said. Don't mind him, he said, he doesn't know you. I reminded him that I wasn't in the habit of staying more than two or three minutes with anyone and that the sea did not agree with me. He seemed deeply grieved to hear it. So you won't come, he said. But to my amazement I got up on the ass and off we went, in the shade of the red chestnuts springing from the sidewalk. I held the ass by the mane, one hand in front of the other. The little boys jeered and threw stones, but their aim was poor, for they only hit me once, on the hat. A policeman stopped us and accused us of disturbing the peace. My friend replied that we were as nature had made us, the boys too were as nature had made them. It was inevitable, under these conditions, that the peace should be disturbed from time to time. Let us continue on our way, he said, and order will soon be restored throughout your beat. We followed the quiet, dustwhite inland roads with their hedges of hawthorn and fuchsia and their footpaths fringed with wild grass and daisies. Night fell. The ass carried me right to the mouth of the cave, for in the dark I could not have found my way down the path winding steeply to the sea. Then he climbed back to his pasture.

I don't know how long I stayed there. The cave was nicely arranged, I must say. I treated my crablice with salt water and seaweed, but a lot of nits must have survived. I put compresses of seaweed on my skull, which gave me great relief, but not for long. I lay in the cave and sometimes looked out at the horizon. I saw above me a vast trembling expanse without islands or promontories. At night a light shone into the cave at regular intervals. It was here I found the phial in my pocket. It was not broken, for the glass was not real glass. I thought Mr Weir had confiscated all my belongings. My host was out most of the time. He fed me on fish. It is easy for a man, a proper man, to live in a cave, far from everybody. He invited me to stay as long as I liked. If I preferred to be alone he would gladly prepare another cave for me farther on. He would bring me food every day and drop in from time to time to make sure I was all right and needed nothing. He was kind. Unfortunately I did not need kindness. You wouldn't know of a lake dwelling? I said. I couldn't bear the sea, its splashing and heaving, its tides and general convulsiveness. The wind at least sometimes stops. My hands and feet felt as though they were full of ants. This kept me awake for hours on end. If I stayed here something awful would happen to me, I said, and a lot of good that would do me. You'd get drowned, he said. Yes, I said, or I'd jump off the cliff. And to think I couldn't live anywhere else, he said, in my cabin in the mountains I was very unhappy. Your cabin in the mountains? I said. He repeated the story of his cabin in the mountains, I had forgotten it, it was as though I were hearing it for the first time. I asked him if he still had it. He replied he had not seen it since the day he fled from it, but that he believed it was still there, a little decayed no doubt. But when he urged me to take the key I refused, saying I had other plans. You will always find me here, he said, if you ever need me. Ah people. He gave me his knife.

What he called his cabin was a sort of wooden shed. The door had been removed, for firewood, or for some other purpose. The glass had disappeared from the window. The roof had fallen in at several places. The interior was divided, by the remains of a partition, into two unequal parts. If there had been any furniture it was gone. The vilest acts had been committed on the ground and against the walls. The floor was strewn with excrements, both human and animal, with condoms and vomit. In a cowpad a heart had been traced, pierced by an arrow. And yet there was nothing to attract tourists. I noticed the remains of abandoned nosegays. They had been greedily gathered, carried for miles, then thrown away, because they were cumbersome or already withered. This was the dwelling to which I had been offered the key.

The scene was the familiar one of grandeur and desolation.

Nevertheless it was a roof over my head. I rested on a bed of ferns, gathered at great labour with my own hands. One day I couldn't get up. The cow saved me. Goaded by the icy mist she came in search of shelter. It was probably not the first time. She can't have seen me. I tried to suck her, without much success. Her udder was covered with dung. I took off my hat and, summoning all my energy, began to milk her into it. The milk fell to the ground and was lost, but I said to myself, No matter, it's free. She dragged me across the floor, stopping from time to time only to kick me. I didn't know our cows too could be so inhuman. She must have recently been milked. Clutching the dug with one hand I kept my hat under it with the other. But in the end she prevailed. For she dragged me across the threshold and out into the giant streaming ferns, where I was forced to let go.

As I drank the milk I reproached myself with what

I had done. I could no longer count on this cow and she would warn the others. More master of myself I might have made a friend of her. She would have come every day, perhaps accompanied by other cows. I might have learnt to make butter, even cheese. But I said to myself, No, all is for the best.

Once on the road it was all downhill. Soon there were carts, but they all refused to take me up. In other clothes, with another face, they might have taken me up. I must have changed since my expulsion from the basement. The face notably seemed to have attained its climacteric. The humble, ingenuous smile would no longer come, nor the expression of candid misery, showing the stars and the distaff. I summoned them, but they would not come. A mask of dirty old hairy leather, with two holes and a slit, it was too far gone for the old trick of please your honour and God reward you and pity upon me. It was disastrous. What would I crawl with in future? I lay down on the side of the road and began to writhe each time I heard a cart approaching. That was so they would not think I was sleeping or resting. I tried to groan, Help! Help! But the tone that came out was that of polite conversation. My hour was not yet come and I could no longer groan. The last time I had cause to groan I had groaned as well as ever, and no heart within miles of me to melt. What was to become of me? I said to myself, I'll learn again. I lay down across the road at a narrow place, so that the carts could not pass without passing over my body, with one wheel at least, or two if there were four. But the day came when, looking round me, I was in the suburbs, and from there to the old haunts it was not far, beyond the stupid hope of rest or less pain.

So I covered the lower part of my face with a black rag and went and begged at a sunny corner. For it seemed to me my eyes were not completely spent, thanks perhaps to the dark glasses my tutor had given me. He had given me the *Ethics* of Geulincx. They were a man's glasses, I was a child. They found him dead, crumpled up in the water closet, his clothes in awful disorder, struck down by an infarctus. Ah what peace. The *Ethics* had his name (Ward) on the fly-leaf, the glasses had belonged to him. The bridge, at the time I am speaking of, was of brass wire, of the kind used to hang pictures and big mirrors, and two long black ribbons served as wings. I wound them round my ears and then down under my chin where I tied them together. The lenses had suffered, from rubbing in my pocket against each other and against the other objects there. I thought Mr Weir had confiscated all my belongings. But I had no further need of these glasses and used them merely to soften the glare of the sun. I should never have mentioned them. The rag gave me a lot of trouble. I got it in the end from the lining of my greatcoat, no, I had no greatcoat now, of my coat then. The result was a grey rag rather than a black, perhaps even chequered, but I had to make do with it. Till afternoon I held my face raised towards the southern sky, then towards the western till night. The bowl gave me a lot of trouble. I couldn't use my hat because of my skull. As for holding out my hand, that was quite out of the question. So I got a tin and hung it from a button of my greatcoat, what's the matter with me, of my coat, at pubis level. It did not hang plumb, it leaned respectfully towards the passer-by, he had only to drop his mite. But that obliged him to come up close to me, he was in danger of touching me. In the end I got a bigger tin, a kind of big tin box, and I placed it on the sidewalk at my feet. But people who give alms don't much care to toss them, there's something contemptuous about this gesture which is repugnant to sensitive natures. To say nothing of their having to aim. They are prepared to give, but not for their gift to go rolling under the passing feet or under the passing wheels, to be picked up perhaps by some undeserving person. So they don't give. There are those, to be sure, who stoop, but generally speaking people who give alms don't much care to stoop. What they like above all is to sight the wretch from afar, get ready their penny, drop it in their stride and hear the God bless you dying away in the distance. Personally I never said that, nor anything like it, I wasn't much of a believer, but I did make a noise with my mouth. In the end I got a kind of board or tray and tied it to my neck and waist. It jutted out just at the right height, pocket height, and its edge was far enough from my person for the coin to be bestowed without danger. Some days I strewed it with flowers, petals, buds and that herb which men call fleabane, I believe, in a word whatever I could find. I didn't go out of my way to look for them, but all the pretty things of this description that came my way were for the board. They must have thought I loved nature. Most of the time I looked up at the sky, but without focussing it, for why focus it? Most of the time it was a mixture of white, blue and grey, and then at evening all the evening colours. I felt it weighing softly on my face, I rubbed my face against it, one cheek after the other, turning my head from side to side. Now and then to rest my neck I dropped my head on my chest. Then I could see the board in the distance, a haze of many colours. I leaned against the wall, but without nonchalance, I shifted my weight from one foot to the other and my hands clutched the lapels of my coat. To beg with your hands in your pockets makes a bad impression, it irritates the workers, especially in winter. You should never wear gloves either. There were guttersnipes who swept away all I had earned, under cover of giving me a coin. It was to buy sweets. I unbuttoned my trousers discreetly to scratch myself. I scratched myself in an upward direction, with four nails. I pulled on the hairs, to get relief. It passed the time, time flew when I scratched myself. Real scratching is superior to masturbation, in my opinion. One can masturbate up to the age of seventy, and even beyond, but in the end it becomes a mere habit. Whereas to scratch myself properly I would have needed a dozen hands. I itched all over, on the privates, in the bush up to the navel, under the arms, in the arse, and then patches of eczema and psoriasis that I could set raging merely by thinking of them. It was in the arse I had the most pleasure. I stuck my forefinger up to the knuckle. Later, if I had to shit, the pain was atrocious. But I hardly shat any more. Now and then a flying machine flew by, sluggishly it seemed to me. Often at the end of the day I discovered the leg of my trousers all wet. That must have been the dogs. I personally pissed very little. If by chance the need came on me a little squirt in my fly was enough to relieve it. Once at my post I did not leave it till nightfall. I had no appetite, God tempered the wind to me. After work I bought a bottle of milk and drank it in the evening in the shed. Better still, I got a little boy to buy it for me, always the same, they wouldn't serve me, I don't know why. I gave him a penny for his pains. One day I witnessed a strange scene. Normally I didn't see a great deal. I didn't hear a great deal either. I didn't pay attention. Strictly speaking I wasn't there. Strictly speaking I believe I've never been anywhere. But that day I must have come back. For some time past a sound had been scarifying me. I did not investigate the cause, for I said to myself, It's going to stop. But as it did not stop I had no choice but to find out the cause. It was a man perched on the roof of a car and haranguing the passers-by. That at least was my interpretation. He was bellowing so loud that snatches of his discourse reached my ears. Union . . . brothers . . . Marx . . . capital . . . bread and butter . . . love. It was all Greek to me. The car was drawn up against the kerb, just in front of me, I saw the orator from behind. All of a sudden he turned and pointed at me, as at an exhibit. Look at this down and out, he vociferated, this leftover. If he doesn't go down on all fours, it's for fear of being impounded. Old, lousy, rotten, ripe for the muckheap. And there are a thousand like him, worse than him, ten thousand, twenty thousand—. A voice, Thirty thousand. Every day you pass them by, resumed the orator, and when you have backed a winner you fling them a farthing. Do you ever think? The voice, God forbid. A penny, resumed the orator, tuppence—. The voice, Thruppence. It never enters your head, resumed the orator, that your charity is a crime, an incentive to slavery, stultification and organized murder. Take a good look at this living corpse. You may say it's his own fault. Ask him if it's his own fault. The voice, Ask him yourself. Then he bent forward and took me to task. I had perfected my board. It now consisted of two boards hinged together, which enabled me, when my work was done, to fold it and carry it under my arm. I liked doing little odd jobs. So I took off the rag, pocketed the few coins I had earned, untied the board, folded it and put it under my arm. Do you hear me, you crucified bastard! cried the orator. Then I went away, although it was still light. But generally speaking it was a quiet corner, busy but not overcrowded, thriving and well-frequented. He must have been a religious fanatic, I could find no other explanation. Perhaps he was an escaped lunatic. He had a nice face, a little on the red side.

I did not work every day. I had practically no expenses. I even managed to put a little aside, for my very last days. The days I did not work I spent lying in the shed. The shed was on a private estate, or what had once been a private estate, on the riverside. This estate, the main entrance to which opened on a narrow, dark and silent street, was enclosed with a wall, except of course on the river front, which marked its northern boundary for a distance of about thirty yards. From the last quays beyond the water the eyes rose to a confusion of low houses, wasteland, hoardings, chimneys, steeples and towers. A kind of parade ground was also to be seen, where soldiers played football all the year round. Only the ground-floor windows—no, I can't. The estate seemed abandoned. The gates were locked and the paths were overgrown with grass. Only the ground-floor windows had shutters. The others were sometimes lit at night, faintly, now one, now another. At least that was my impression. Perhaps it was reflected light. In this shed, the day I adopted it, I found a boat, upside down. I righted it, chocked it up with stones and pieces of wood, took out the thwarts and made my bed inside. The rats had difficulty in getting at me, because of the bulge of the hull. And yet they longed to. Just think of it, living flesh, for in spite of everything I was still living flesh. I had lived too long among rats, in my chance dwellings, to share the dread they inspire in the vulgar. I even had a soft spot in my heart for them. They came with such confidence towards me, it seemed without the least repugnance. They made their toilet with catlike gestures. Toads at evening, motionless for hours, lap flies from the air. They like to squat where cover ends and open air begins, they favour thresholds. But I had to contend now with water rats, exceptionally lean and ferocious. So I made a kind of lid with stray boards. It's incredible the number of boards I've come across in my lifetime, I never needed a board but there it was, I had only to stoop and pick it up. I liked doing little odd jobs, no, not particularly, I didn't mind. It completely covered the boat, I'm referring again to the lid. I pushed it a little towards the stern, climbed into the boat by the bow, crawled to the stern, raised my feet and pushed the lid back to the bow till it covered me completely. But what did my feet push against? They pushed against a cross bar I nailed to the lid for that purpose, I liked these little odd jobs. But it was better to climb into the boat by the stern and pull back the lid with my hands till it completely covered me, then push it forward in the same way when I wanted to get out. As holds for my hands I planted two spikes just where I needed them. These little odds and ends of carpentry, if I may so describe it, carried out with whatever tools and material I chanced to find, gave me a certain pleasure. I knew it would soon be the end, so I played the part, you know, the part of—how shall I say, I don't know. I was comfortable enough in this boat, I must say. The lid fitted so well I had to pierce a hole. It's no good closing your eyes, you must leave them open in the dark, that is my opinion. I am not speaking of sleep, I am speaking of what I believe is called waking. In any case, I slept very little at this period, I wasn't sleepy, or I was too sleepy, I don't know, or I was afraid, I don't know. Flat then on my back I saw nothing except, dimly, just above my head, through the tiny chinks, the grey light of the shed. To see nothing at all, no, that's too much. I heard faintly the cries of the gulls ravening about the mouth of the sewer near by. In a spew of yellow foam, if my memory serves me right, the filth gushed into the river and the slush of birds above screaming with hunger and fury. I heard the lapping of water against the slip and against the bank and the other sound, so different, of open wave, I heard it too. I too, when I moved, felt less boat than wave, or so it seemed to me, and my stillness was the stillness of eddies. That may seem impossible. The rain too, I often heard it, for it often rained. Sometimes a drop, falling through the roof of the shed, exploded on me. All that composed a rather liquid world. And then of course there was the voice of the wind or rather those, so various, of its playthings. But what does it amount to? Howling, soughing, moaning, sighing. What I would have liked was hammer strokes, bang bang bang, clanging in the desert. I let farts to be sure, but hardly ever a real crack, they oozed out with a sucking noise, melted in the mighty never. I don't know how long I stayed there. I was very snug in my box, I must say. It seemed to me I had grown more independent of recent years. That no one came any more, that no one could come any more, to ask me if I was all right and needed nothing, distressed me then but little. I was all right, yes, quite so, and the fear of getting worse was less with me. As for my needs, they had dwindled as it were to my dimensions and become, if I may say so, of so exquisite a quality as to exclude all thought of succour. To know I had a being, however faint and false, outside of me, had once had the power to stir my heart. You become unsociable, it's inevitable. It's enough to make you wonder sometimes if you are on the right planet. Even the words desert you, it's as bad as that. Perhaps it's the moment when the vessels stop communicating, you know, the vessels. There you are still between the two murmurs, it must be the same old song as ever, but Christ you wouldn't think so. There were times when I wanted to push away the lid and get out of the boat and couldn't, I was so indolent and weak, so content deep down where I was. I felt them hard upon me, the icy, tumultuous streets, the terrifying faces, the noises that slash, pierce, claw, bruise. So I waited till the desire to shit, or even to piss, lent me wings. I did not want to dirty my nest! And yet it sometimes happened, and even more and more often. Arched and rigid I edged down my trousers and turned a little on my side, just enough to free the hole. To contrive a little kingdom, in the midst of the universal muck, then shit on it, ah that was me all over. The excrements were me too, I know, I know, but all the same. Enough, enough, the next thing I was having visions, I who never did, except sometimes in my sleep, who never had, real visions, I'd remember, except perhaps as a child, my myth will have it so. I knew they were visions because it was night and I was alone in my boat. What else could they have been? So I was in my boat and gliding on the waters. I didn't have to row, the ebb was carrying me out. Anyway I saw no oars, they must have taken them away. I had a board, the remains of a thwart perhaps, which I used when I came too close to the bank, or when a pier came bearing down on me or a barge at its moorings. There were stars in the sky, quite a few. I didn't know what the weather was doing, I was neither cold nor warm and all seemed calm. The banks receded more and more, it was inevitable, soon I saw them no more. The lights grew fainter and fewer as the river widened. There on the land men were sleeping, bodies were gathering strength for the toil and joys of the morrow. The boat was not gliding now, it was tossing, buffeted by the choppy waters of the bay. All seemed calm and yet foam was washing aboard. Now the sea air was all about me, I had no other shelter than the land, and what does it amount to, the shelter of the land, at such a time. I saw the beacons, four in all, including a lightship. I knew them well, even as a child I had known them well. It was evening, I was with my father on a height, he held my hand. I would have liked him to draw me close with a gesture of protective love, but his mind was on other things. He also taught me the names of the mountains. But to have done with these visions I also saw the lights of the buoys, the sea seemed full of them, red and green, and to my surprise even yellow. And on the slopes of the mountain, now rearing its unbroken bulk behind the town, the fires turned from gold to red, from red to gold. I knew what it was, it was the gorse burning. How often I had set a match to it myself, as a child. And hours later, back in my home, before I climbed into bed, I watched from my high window the fires I had lit. That night then, all aglow with distant fires, on sea, on land and in the sky, I drifted with the currents and the tides. I noticed that my hat was tied, with a string I suppose, to my buttonhole. I got up from my seat in the stern and a great clanking was heard. That was the chain. One end was fastened to the bow and the other round my waist. I must have pierced a hole beforehand in the floor-boards, for there I was down on my knees prying out the plug with my knife. The hole was small and the water rose slowly. It would take a good half hour, everything included, barring accidents. Back now in the stern-sheets, my legs stretched out, my back well propped against the sack stuffed with grass I used as a cushion, I swallowed my calmative. The sea, the sky, the mountains and the islands closed in and crushed me in a mighty systole, then scattered to the uttermost confines of space. The memory came faint and cold of the story I might have told, a story in the likeness of my life, I mean without the courage to end or the strength to go on.

—Translated by Richard Seaver
in collaboration with the author.

TEXTS FOR NOTHING

Translated by the author

1

Suddenly, no, at last, long last, I couldn't any more, I couldn't go on. Someone said, You can't stay here. I couldn't stay there and I couldn't go on. I'll describe the place, that's unimportant. The top, very flat, of a mountain, no, a hill, but so wild, so wild, enough. Quag, heath up to the knees, faint sheep-tracks, troughs scooped deep by the rains. It was far down in one of these I was lying, out of the wind. Glorious prospect, but for the mist that blotted out everything, valleys, loughs, plain and sea. How can I go on, I shouldn't have begun, no, I had to begin. Someone said, perhaps the same, What possessed you to come? I could have stayed in my den, snug and dry, I couldn't. My den, I'll describe it, no, I can't. It's simple, I can do nothing any more, that's what you think. I say to the body, Up with you now, and I can feel it struggling, like an old hack foundered in the street, struggling no more, struggling again, till it gives up. I say to the head, Leave it alone, stay quiet, it stops breathing, then pants on worse than ever. I am far from all that wrangle, I shouldn't bother with it, I need nothing, neither to go on nor to stay where I am, it's truly all one to me, I should turn away from it all, away from the body, away from the head, let them work it out between them, let them cease, I can't, it's I would have to cease. Ah yes, we seem to be more than one, all deaf, not even, gathered together for life. Another said, or the same, or the first, they all have the same voice, the same ideas, All you had to do was stay at home. Home. They wanted me to go home. My dwelling-place. But for the mist, with good eyes, with a telescope, I could see it from here. It's not just tiredness, I'm not just tired, in spite of the climb. It's not that I want to stay here either. I had heard tell, I must have heard tell of the view, the distant sea in hammered lead, the so-called golden vale so often sung, the double valleys, the glacial loughs, the city in its haze, it was all on every tongue. Who are these people anyway? Did they follow me up here, go before me, come with me? I am down in the hole the centuries have dug, centuries of filthy weather, flat on my face on the dark earth sodden with the creeping saffron waters it slowly drinks. They are up above, all round me, as in a graveyard. I can't raise my eyes to them, what a pity, I wouldn't see their faces, their legs perhaps, plunged in the heath. Do they see me, what can they see of me? Perhaps there is no one left, perhaps they are all gone, sickened. I listen and it's the same thoughts I hear, I mean the same as ever, strange. To think in the valley the sun is blazing all down the ravelled sky. How long have I been here, what a question, I've often wondered. And often I could answer, An hour, a month, a year, a century, depending on what I meant by here, and me, and being, and there I never went looking for extravagant meanings, there I never much varied, only the here would sometimes seem to vary. Or I said, I can't have been here long, I wouldn't have held out. I hear the curlews, that means close of day, fall of night, for that's the way with curlews, silent all day, then crying when the darkness gathers, that's the way with those wild creatures and so short-lived, compared with me. And that other question I know so well too, What possessed you to come?, unanswerable, so that I answered, To change, or, It's not me, or, Chance, or again, To see, or again, years of great sun, Fate, I feel that other coming, let it come, it won't catch me napping. All is noise, unending suck of black sopping peat, surge of giant ferns, heathery gulfs of quiet where the wind drowns, my life and its old jingles. To change, to see, no, there's no more to see, I've seen it all, till my eyes are blear, nor to get away from harm, the harm is done, one day the harm was done, the day my feet dragged me out that must go their ways, that I let go their ways and drag me here, that's what possessed me to come. And what I'm doing, all-important, breathing in and out and saying, with words like smoke, I can't go, I can't stay, let's see what happens next. And in the way of sensation? My God I can't complain, it's himself all right, only muffled, like buried in snow, less the warmth, less the drowse, I can follow them well, all the voices, all the parts, fairly well, the cold is eating me, the wet too, at least I presume so, I'm far. My rheumatism in any case is no more than a memory, it hurts me no more than my mother's did, when it hurt her. Eye ravening patient in the haggard vulture face, perhaps it's carrion time. I'm up there and I'm down here, under my gaze, foundered, eyes closed, ear cupped against the sucking peat, we're of one mind, all of one mind, always were, deep down, we're fond of one another, we're sorry for one another, but there it is, there's nothing we can do for one another. One thing at least is certain, in an hour it will be too late, in half-an-hour it will be night, and yet it's not, not certain, what is not certain, absolutely certain, that night prevents what day permits, for those who know how to go about it, who have the will to go about it, and the strength, the strength to try again. Yes, it will be night, the mist will clear, I know my mist, for all my distraction, the wind freshen and the whole night sky open over the mountain, with its lights, including the Bears, to guide me once again on my way, let's wait for night. All mingles, times and tenses, at first I only had been here, now I'm here still, soon I won't be here yet, toiling up the slope, or in the bracken by the wood, it's larch, I don't try to understand, I'll never try to understand any more, that's what you think, for the moment I'm here, always have been, always shall be, I won't be afraid of the big words any more, they are not big. I don't remember coming, I can't go, all my little company, my eyes are closed and I feel the wet humus harsh against my cheek, my hat is gone, it can't be gone far, or the wind has swept it away, I was attached to it. Sometimes it's the sea, other times the mountains, often it was the forest, the city, the plain too, I've flirted with the plain too, I've given myself up for dead all over the place, of hunger, of old age, murdered, drowned, and then for no reason, of tedium, nothing like breathing your last to put new life in you, and then the rooms, natural death, tucked up in bed, smothered in household gods, and always muttering, the same old mutterings, the same old stories, the same old questions and answers, no malice in me, hardly any, stultior stultissimo, never an imprecation, not such a fool, or else it's gone from mind. Yes, to the end, always muttering, to lull me and keep me company, and all ears always, all ears for the old stories, as when my father took me on his knee and read me the one about Joe Breem, or Breen, the son of a lighthouse keeper, evening after evening, all the long winter through. A tale, it was a tale for children, it all happened on a rock, in the storm, the mother was dead and the gulls came beating against the light, Joe jumped into the sea, that's all I remember, a knife between his teeth, did what was to be done and came back, that's all I remember this evening, it ended happily, it began unhappily and it ended happily, every evening, a comedy, for children. Yes, I was my father and I was my son, I asked myself questions and answered as best I could, I had it told to me evening after evening, the same old story I knew by heart and couldn't believe, or we walked together, hand in hand, silent, sunk in our worlds, each in his worlds, the hands forgotten in each other. That's how I've held out till now. And this evening again it seems to be working, I'm in my arms, I'm holding myself in my arms, without much tenderness, but faithfully, faithfully. Sleep now, as under that ancient lamp, all twined together, tired out with so much talking, so much listening, so much toil and play.

2

Above is the light, the elements, a kind of light, sufficient to see by, the living find their ways, without too much trouble, avoid one another, unite, avoid the obstacles, without too much trouble, seek with their eyes, close their eyes, halting, without halting, among the elements, the living. Unless it has changed, unless it has ceased. The things too must still be there, a little more worn, a little even less, many still standing where they stood in the days of their indifference. Here you are under a different glass, not long habitable either, it's time to leave it. You are there, there it is, where you are will never long be habitable. Go then, no, better stay, for where would you go, now that you know? Back above? There are limits. Back in that kind of light. See the cliffs again, be again between the cliffs and the sea, reeling shrinking with your hands over your ears, headlong, innocent, suspect, noxious. Seek, by the excessive light of night, a demand commensurate with the offer, and go to ground empty-handed at the old crack of day. See Mother Calvet again, creaming off the garbage before the nightmen come. She must still be there. With her dog and her skeletal baby buggy. What could be more endurable? She wavered through the night, a kind of trident in her hand, muttering and ejaculating, Your highness! Your honour! The dog tottered on its hindlegs begging, hooked its paws over the rim of the can and snouted round with her in the muck. It got in her way, she cursed it for a lousy cur and let it have its way. There's a good memory. Mother Calvet. She knew what she liked, perhaps even what she would have liked. And beauty, strength, intelligence, the latest, daily, action, poetry, all one price for one and all. If only it could be wiped from knowledge. To have suffered under that miserable light, what a blunder. It let nothing show, it would have gone out, nothing terrible, nothing showed, of the true affair, it would have snuffed out. And now here, what now here, one enormous second, as in Paradise, and the mind slow, slow, nearly stopped. And yet it's changing, something is changing, it must be in the head, slowly in the head the ragdoll rotting, perhaps we're in a head, it's as dark as in a head before the worms get at it, ivory dungeon. The words too, slow, slow, the subject dies before it comes to the verb, words are stopping too. Better off then than when life was babble? That's it, that's it, the bright side. And the absence of others, does that count for so little? Pah others, that's nothing, others never inconvenienced anyone, and there must be a few here too, other others, invisible, mute, what does it matter. It's true you hid from them, hugged their walls, true, you miss that here, you miss the derivatives, here it's pure ache, pah you were saying that above and you a living mustard-plaster. So long as the words keep coming nothing will have changed, there are the old words out again. Utter, there's nothing else, utter, void yourself of them, here as always, nothing else. But they are failing, true, that's the change, they are failing, that's bad, bad. Or it's the dread of coming to the last, of having said all, your all, before the end, no, for that will be the end, the end of all, not certain. To need to groan and not be able, Jesus, better ration yourself, watch out for the genuine deathpangs, some are deceptive, you think you're home, start howling and revive, health-giving howls, better be silent, it's the only method, if you want to end, not a word but smiles, end rent with stifled imprecations, burst with speechlessness, all is possible, what now. Perhaps above it's summer, a summer Sunday, Mr Joly is in the belfry, he has wound up the clock, now he's ringing the bells. Mr Joly. He had only one leg and a half. Sunday. It was folly to be abroad. The roads were crawling with them, the same roads so often kind. Here at least none of that, no talk of a creator and nothing very definite in the way of a creation. Dry, it's possible, or wet, or slime, as before matter took ill. Is this stuff air that permits you to suffocate still, almost audibly at times, it's possible, a kind of air. What exactly is going on, exactly, ah old xanthic laugh, no, farewell mirth, good riddance, it was never droll. No, but one more memory, one last memory, it may help, to abort again. Piers pricking his oxen o'er the plain, no, for at the end of the furrow, before turning to the next, he raised his eyes to the sky and said, Bright again too early. And sure enough, soon after, the snow. In other words the night was black, when it fell at last, but no, strange, it wasn't, in spite of the buried sky. The way was long that led back to the den, over the fields, a winding way, it must still be there. When it comes to the top of the cliff it springs, some might think blindly, but no, wilily, like a goat, in hairpin zigzags towards the shore. Never had the sea so thundered from afar, the sea beneath the snow, though superlatives have lost most of their charm. The day had not been fruitful, as was only natural, considering the season, that of the very last leeks. It was none the less the return, to what no matter, the return, unscathed, always a matter for wonder. What happened? Is that the question? An encounter? Bang! No. Level with the farm of the Graves brothers a brief halt, opposite the lamplit window. A glow, red, afar, at night, in winter, that's worth having, that must have been worth having. There, it's done, it ends there, I end there. A far memory, far from the last, it's possible, the legs seem to be still working. A pity hope is dead. No. How one hoped above, on and off. With what diversity.

3

Leave, I was going to say leave all that. What matter who's speaking, someone said what matter who's speaking. There's going to be a departure, I'll be there, I won't miss it, it won't be me, I'll be here, I'll say I'm far from here, it won't be me, I won't say anything, there's going to be a story, someone's going to try and tell a story. Yes, no more denials, all is false, there is no one, it's understood, there is nothing, no more phrases, let us be dupes, dupes of every time and tense, until it's done, all past and done, and the voices cease, it's only voices, only lies. Here, depart from here and go elsewhere, or stay here, but coming and going. Start by stirring, there must be a body, as of old, I don't deny it, no more denials, I'll say I'm a body, stirring back and forth, up and down, as required. With a cluther of limbs and organs, all that is needed to live again, to hold out a little time, I'll call that living, I'll say it's me, I'll get standing, I'll stop thinking, I'll be too busy, getting standing, staying standing, stirring about, holding out, getting to tomorrow, tomorrow week, that will be ample, a week will be ample, a week in spring, that puts the jizz in you. It's enough to will it, I'll will it, will me a body, will me a head, a little strength, a little courage, I'm starting now, a week is soon served, then back here, this inextricable place, far from the days, the far days, it's not going to be easy. And why, come to think, no no, leave it, no more of that, don't listen to it all, don't say it all, it's all old, all one, once and for all. There you are now on your feet, I give you my word, I swear they're yours, I swear it's mine, get to work with your hands, palp your skull, seat of the understanding, without which nix, then the rest, the lower regions, you'll be needing them, and say what you're like, have a guess, what kind of man, there has to be a man, or a woman, feel between your legs, no need of beauty, nor of vigour, a week's a short stretch, no one's going to love you, don't be alarmed. No, not like that, too sudden, I gave myself a start. And to start with stop palpitating, no one's going to kill you, no one's going to love you and no one's going to kill you, perhaps you'll emerge in the high depression of Gobi, you'll feel at home there. I'll wait for you here, no, I am alone, I alone am, this time it's I must go. I know how I'll do it, I'll be a man, there's nothing else for it, a kind of man, a kind of old tot, I'll have a nanny, I'll be her sweet pet, she'll give me her hand, to cross over, she'll let me loose in the Green, I'll be good, I'll sit quiet as a mouse in a corner and comb my beard, I'll tease it out, to look more bonny, a little more bonny, if only it could be like that. She'll say to me, Come, doty, it's time for bye-bye. I'll have no responsibility, she'll have all the responsibility, her name will be Bibby, I'll call her Bibby, if only it could be like that. Come, ducky, it's time for yum-yum. Who taught me all I know, I alone, in the old wanderyears, I deduced it all from nature, with the help of an all-in-one, I know it's not me, but it's too late now, too late to deny it, the knowledge is there, the bits and scraps, flickering on and off, turn about, winking on the storm, in league to fool me. Leave it and go, it's time to go, to say so anyway, the moment has come, it's not known why. What matter how you describe yourself, here or elsewhere, fixed or mobile, without form or oblong like man, in the dark or the light of the heavens, I don't know, it seems to matter, it's not going to be easy. And if I went back to where all went out and on from there, no, that would lead nowhere, never led anywhere, the memory of it has gone out too, a great flame and then blackness, a great spasm and then no more weight or traversable space. I tried throwing me off a cliff, collapsing in the street in the midst of mortals, that led nowhere, I gave up. Take the road again that cast me up here, then retrace it, or follow it on, wise advice. That's so that I'll never stir again, dribble on here till time is done, murmuring every ten centuries, It's not me, it's not true, it's not me, I'm far. No no, I'll speak now of the future, I'll speak in the future, as when I used to say, in the night, to myself, Tomorrow I'll put on my dark blue tie, with the yellow stars, and put it on, when night was past. Quick quick before I weep. I'll have a crony, my own vintage, my own bog, a fellow warrior, we'll relive our campaigns and compare our scratches. Quick quick. He'll have served in the navy, perhaps under Jellicoe, while I was potting at the invader from behind a barrel of Guinness, with my arquebuse. We have not long, that's the spirit, in the present, not long to live, it's our positively last winter, halleluiah. We wonder what will carry us off in the end. He's gone in the wind, I in the prostate rather. We envy each other, I envy him, he envies me, occasionally. I catheterize myself, unaided, with trembling hand, bent double in the public pisshouse, under cover of my cloak, people take me for a dirty old man.

He waits for me to finish, sitting on a bench, coughing up his guts, spitting into a snuffbox which no sooner overflows than he empties it in the canal, out of civic-mindedness. We have well deserved of our motherland, she'll get us into the Incurables before we die. We spend our life, it's ours, trying to bring together in the same instant a ray of sunshine and a free bench, in some oasis of public verdure, we've been seized by a love of nature, in our sere and yellow, it belongs to one and all, in places. In a choking murmur he reads out to me from the paper of the day before, he had far far better been the blind one. The sport of kings is our passion, the dogs too, we have no political opinions, simply limply republican. But we also have a soft spot for the Windsors, the Hanoverians, I forget, the Hohenzollerns is it. Nothing human is foreign to us, once we have digested the racing news. No, alone, I'd be better off alone, it would be quicker. He'd nourish me, he had a friend a pork-butcher, he'd ram the ghost back down my gullet with black pudding. With his consolations, allusions to cancer, recollections of imperishable raptures, he'd prevent discouragement from sapping my foundations. And I, instead of concentrating on my own horizons, which might have enabled me to throw them under a lorry, would let my mind be taken off them by his. I'd say to him, Come on, gunner, leave all that, think no more about it, and it's I would think no more about it, besotted with brotherliness. And the obligations! I have in mind particularly the appointments at ten in the morning, hail rain or shine, in front of Duggan's, thronged already with sporting men fevering to get their bets out of harm's way before the bars open. We were, there we are past and gone again, so much the better, so much the better, most punctual I must say. To see the remains of Vincent arriving in sheets of rain, with the brave involuntary swagger of the old tar, his head swathed in a bloody clout and a glitter in his eye, was for the acute observer an example of what man is capable of, in his pursuit of pleasure. With one hand he sustained his sternum, with the heel of the other his spinal column, as if tempted to break into a hornpipe, no, that's all memories, last shifts older than the flood. See what's happening here, where there's no one, where nothing happens, get something to happen here, someone to be here, then put an end to it, have silence, get into silence, or another sound, a sound of other voices than those of life and death, of lives and deaths everyone's but mine, get into my story in order to get out of it, no, that's all meaningless. Is it possible I'll sprout a head at last, all my very own, in which to brew poisons worthy of me, and legs to kick my heels with, I'd be there at last, I could go at last, it's all I ask, no, I can't ask anything. Just the head and the two legs, or one, in the middle, I'd go hopping. Or just the head, nice and round, nice and smooth, no need of lineaments, I'd go rolling, downhill, almost a pure spirit, no, that wouldn't work, all is uphill from here, the leg is unavoidable, or the equivalent, perhaps a few annular joints, contractile, great ground to be covered with them. To set out from Duggan's door, on a spring morning of rain and shine, not knowing if you'll ever get to evening, what's wrong with that? It would be so easy. To be bedded in that flesh or in another, in that arm held by a friendly hand, and in that hand, without arms, without hands, and without soul in those trembling souls, through the crowd, the hoops, the toy balloons, what's wrong with that? I don't know, I'm here, that's all I know, and that it's still not me, it's of that the best has to be made. There is no flesh anywhere, nor any way to die. Leave all that, to want to leave all that, not knowing what that means, all that, it's soon said, soon done, in vain, nothing has stirred, no one has spoken. Here, nothing will happen here, no one will be here, for many a long day. Departures, stories, they are not for tomorrow. And the voices, wherever they come from, have no life in them.

4

Where would I go, if I could go, who would I be, if I could be, what would I say, if I had a voice, who says this, saying it's me? Answer simply, someone answer simply. It's the same old stranger as ever, for whom alone accusative I exist, in the pit of my inexistence, of his, of ours, there's a simple answer. It's not with thinking he'll find me, but what is he to do, living and bewildered, yes, living, say what he may. Forget me, know me not, yes, that would be the wisest, none better able than he. Why this sudden affability after such desertion, it's easy to understand, that's what he says, but he doesn't understand. I'm not in his head, nowhere in his old body, and yet I'm there, for him I'm there, with him, hence all the confusion. That should have been enough for him, to have found me absent, but it's not, he wants me there, with a form and a world, like him, in spite of him, me who am everything, like him who is nothing. And when he feels me void of existence it's of his he would have me void, and vice versa, mad, mad, he's mad. The truth is he's looking for me to kill me, to have me dead like him, dead like the living. He knows all that, but it's no help his knowing it, I don't know it, I know nothing. He protests he doesn't reason and does nothing but reason, crooked, as if that could improve matters. He thinks words fail him, he thinks because words fail him he's on his way to my speechlessness, to being speechless with my speechlessness, he would like it to be my fault that words fail him, of course words fail him. He tells his story every five minutes, saying it is not his, there's cleverness for you. He would like it to be my fault that he has no story, of course he has no story, that's no reason for trying to foist one on me. That's how he reasons, wide of the mark, but wide of what mark, answer us that. He has me say things saying it's not me, there's profundity for you, he has me who say nothing say it's not me. All that is truly crass. If at least he would dignify me with the third person, like his other figments, not he, he'll be satisfied with nothing less than me, for his me. When he had me, when he was me, he couldn't get rid of me quick enough, I didn't exist, he couldn't have that, that was no kind of life, of course I didn't exist, any more than he did, of course it was no kind of life, now he has it, his kind of life, let him lose it, if he wants to be in peace, with a bit of luck. His life, what a mine, what a life, he can't have that, you can't fool him, ergo it's not his, it's not him, what a thought, treat him like that, like a vulgar Molloy, a common Malone, those mere mortals, happy mortals, have a heart, land him in that shit, who never stirred, who is none but me, all things considered, and what things, and how considered, he had only to keep out of it. That's how he speaks, this evening, how he has me speak, how he speaks to himself, how I speak, there is only me, this evening, here, on earth, and a voice that makes no sound because it goes towards none, and a head strewn with arms laid down and corpses fighting fresh, and a body, I nearly forgot. This evening, I say this evening, perhaps it's morning. And all these things, what things, all about me, I won't deny them any more, there's no sense in that any more. If it's nature perhaps it's trees and birds, they go together, water and air, so that all may go on, I don't need to know the details, perhaps I'm sitting under a palm. Or it's a room, with furniture, all that's required to make life comfortable, dark, because of the wall outside the window. What am I doing, talking, having my figments talk, it can only be me. Spells of silence too, when I listen, and hear the local sounds, the world sounds, see what an effort I make, to be reasonable. There's my life, why not, it is one, if you like, if you must, I don't say no, this evening. There has to be one, it seems, once there is speech, no need of a story, a story is not compulsory, just a life, that's the mistake I made, one of the mistakes, to have wanted a story for myself, whereas life alone is enough. I'm making progress, it was time, I'll learn to keep my foul mouth shut before I'm done, if nothing foreseen crops up. But he who somehow comes and goes, unaided from place to place, even though nothing happens to him, true, what of him? I stay here, sitting, if I'm sitting, often I feel sitting, sometimes standing, it's one or the other, or lying down, there's another possibility, often I feel lying down, it's one of the three, or kneeling. What counts is to be in the world, the posture is immaterial, so long as one is on earth. To breathe is all that is required, there is no obligation to ramble, or receive company, you may even believe yourself dead on condition you make no bones about it, what more liberal regimen could be imagined, I don't know, I don't imagine. No point under such circumstances in saying I am somewhere else, someone else, such as I am I have all I need to hand, for to do what, I don't know, all I have to do, there I am on my own again at last, what a relief that must be. Yes, there are moments, like this moment, when I seem almost restored to the feasible. Then it goes, all goes, and I'm far again, with a far story again, I wait for me afar for my story to begin, to end, and again this voice cannot be mine. That's where I'd go, if I could go, that's who I'd be, if I could be.

5

I'm the clerk, I'm the scribe, at the hearings of what cause I know not. Why want it to be mine, I don't want it. There it goes again, that's the first question this evening. To be judge and party, witness and advocate, and he, attentive, indifferent, who sits and notes. It's an image, in my helpless head, where all sleeps, all is dead, not yet born, I don't know, or before my eyes, they see the scene, the lids flicker and it's in. An instant and then they close again, to look inside the head, to try and see inside, to look for me there, to look for someone there, in the silence of quite a different justice, in the toils of that obscure assize where to be is to be guilty. That is why nothing appears, all is silent, one is frightened to be born, no, one wishes one were, so as to begin to die. One, meaning me, it's not the same thing, in the dark where I will in vain to see there can't be any willing. I could get up, take a little turn, I long to, but I won't. I know where I'd go, I'd go into the forest, I'd try and reach the forest, unless that's where I am, I don't know where I am, in any case I stay. I see what it is, I seek to be like the one I seek, in my head, that my head seeks, that I bid my head seek, with its probes, within itself. No, don't pretend to seek, don't pretend to think, just be vigilant, the eyes staring behind the lids, the ears straining for a voice not from without, were it only to sound an instant, to tell another lie. I hear, that must be the voice of reason again, that the vigil is in vain, that I'd be better advised to take a little turn, the way you manoeuvre a tin soldier. And no doubt it's the same voice answers that I can't, I who but a moment ago seemed to think I could, unless it's old shuttlecock sentiment chiming in, full stop, got all that. Why did Pozzo leave home, he had a castle and retainers. Insidious question, to remind me I'm in the dock. Sometimes I hear things that seem for a moment judicious, for a moment I'm sorry they are not mine. Then what a relief, what a relief to know I'm mute for ever, if only it didn't distress me. And deaf, it seems to me sometimes that deaf I'd be less distressed, at being mute, listen to that, what a relief not to have that on my conscience. Ah yes, I hear I have a kind of conscience, and on top of that a kind of sensibility, I trust the orator is not forgetting anything, and without ceasing to listen or drive the old quill I'm afflicted by them, I heard, it's noted. This evening the session is calm, there are long silences when all fix their eyes on me, that's to make me fly off my hinges, I feel on the brink of shrieks, it's noted. Out of the corner of my eye I observe the writing hand, all dimmed and blurred by the—by the reverse of farness. Who are all these people, gentlemen of the long robe, according to the image, but according to it alone, there are others, there will be others, other images, other gentlemen. Shall I never see the sky again, never be free again to come and go, in sunshine and in rain, the answer is no, all answer no, it's well I didn't ask anything, that's the kind of extravagance I envy them, till the echoes die away. The sky,

I've heard—the sky and earth, I've heard great accounts of them, now that's pure word for word, I invent nothing. I've noted, I must have noted many a story with them as setting, they create the atmosphere. Between them where the hero stands a great gulf is fixed, while all about they flow together more and more, till they meet, so that he finds himself as it were under glass, and yet with no limit to his movements in all directions, let him understand who can, that is no part of my attributions. The sea too, I am conversant with the sea too, it belongs to the same family, I have even gone to the bottom more than once, under various assumed names, don't make me laugh, if only I could laugh, all would vanish, all what, who knows, all, me, it's noted. Yes, I see the scene, I see the hand, it comes creeping out of shadow, the shadow of my head, then scurries back, no connexion with me. Like a little creepy crawly it ventures out an instant, then goes back in again, the things one has to listen to, I say it as I hear it. It's the clerk's hand, is he entitled to the wig, I don't know, formerly perhaps. What do I do when silence falls, with rhetorical intent, or denoting lassitude, perplexity, consternation, I rub to and fro against my lips, where they meet, the first knuckle of my forefinger, but it's the head that moves, the hand rests, it's to such details the liar pins his hopes. That's the way this evening, tomorrow will be different, perhaps I'll appear before the council, before the justice of him who is all love, unforgiving and justly so, but subject to strange indulgences, the accused will be my soul, I prefer that, perhaps someone will ask pity for my soul, I mustn't miss that, I won't be there, neither will God, it doesn't matter, we'll be represented. Yes, it can't be much longer now, I haven't been damned for what seems an eternity, yes, but sufficient unto the day, this evening I'm the scribe. This evening, it's always evening, always spoken of as evening, even when it's morning, it's to make me think night is at hand, bringer of rest. The first thing would be to believe I'm there, if I could do that I'd lap up the rest, there'd be none more credulous than me, if I were there. But I am, it's not possible otherwise, just so, it's not possible, it doesn't need to be possible. It's tiring, very tiring, in the same breath to win and lose, with concomitant emotions, one's heart is not of stone, to record the doom, don the black cap and collapse in the dock, very tiring, in the long run, I'm tired of it, I'd be tired of it, if I were me. It's a game, it's getting to be a game, I'm going to rise and go, if it's not me it will be someone, a phantom, long live all our phantoms, those of the dead, those of the living and those of those who are not born. I'll follow him, with my sealed eyes, he needs no door, needs no thought, to issue from this imaginary head, mingle with air and earth and dissolve, little by little, in exile. Now I'm haunted, let them go, one by one, let the last desert me and leave me empty, empty and silent. It's they murmur my name, speak to me of me, speak of a me, let them go and speak of it to others, who will not believe them either, or who will believe them too. Theirs all these voices, like a rattling of chains in my head, rattling to me that I have a head. That's where the court sits this evening, in the depths of that vaulty night, that's where I'm clerk and scribe, not understanding what I hear, not knowing what I write. That's where the council will be tomorrow, prayers will be offered for my soul, as for that of one dead, as for that of an infant dead in its dead mother, that it may not go to Limbo, sweet thing theology. It will be another evening, all happens at evening, but it will be the same night, it too has its evenings, its mornings and its evenings, there's a pretty conception, it's to make me think day is at hand, disperser of phantoms. And now birds, the first birds, what's this new trouble now, don't forget the question-mark. It must be the end of the session, it's been calm, on the whole. Yes, that's sometimes the way, there are suddenly birds and all goes silent, an instant. But the phantoms come back, it's in vain they go abroad, mingle with the dying, they come back and slip into the coffin, no bigger than a matchbox, it's they have taught me all I know, about things above, and all I'm said to know about me, they want to create me, they want to make me, like the bird the birdikin, with larvae she fetches from afar, at the peril—I nearly said at the peril of her life! But sufficient unto the day, those are other minutes. Yes, one begins to be very tired, very tired of one's toil, very tired of one's quill, it falls, it's noted.

6

How are the intervals filled between these apparitions? Do my keepers snatch a little rest and sleep before setting about me afresh, how would that be? That would be very natural, to enable them to get back their strength. Do they play cards, the odd rubber, bowls, to recruit their spirits, are they entitled to a little recreation? I would say no, if I had a say, no recreation, just a short break, with something cold, even though they should not feel inclined, in the interests of their health. They like their work, I feel it in my bones! No, I mean how filled for me, they don't come into this. Wretched acoustics this evening, the merest scraps, literally. The news, do you remember the news, the latest news, in slow letters of light, above Piccadilly Circus, in the fog? Where were you standing, in the doorway of the little tobacconist's closed for the night on the corner of Glasshouse Street was it, no, you don't remember, and for cause. Sometimes that's how it is, in a way, the eyes take over, and the silence, the sighs, like the sighs of sadness weary with crying, or old, that suddenly feels old and sighs for itself, for the happy days, the long days, when it cried it would never perish, but it's far from common, on the whole. My keepers, why keepers, I'm in no danger of stirring an inch, ah I see, it's to make me think I'm a prisoner, frantic with corporeality, rearing to get out and away. Other times it's male nurses, white from head to foot, even their shoes are white, and then it's another story, but the burden is the same. Other times it's like ghouls, naked and soft as worm, they grovel round me gloating on the corpse, but I have no more success dead than dying. Other times it's great clusters of bones, dangling and knocking with a clatter of castanets, it's clean and gay like coons, I'd join them with a will if it could be here and now, how is it nothing is ever here and now? It's varied, my life is varied, I'll never get anywhere. I know, there is no one here, neither me nor anyone else, but some things are better left unsaid, so I say nothing. Elewhere perhaps, by all means, elsewhere, what elsewhere can there be to this infinite here? I know, if my head could think I'd find a way out, in my head, like so many others, and out of worse than this, the world would be there again, in my head, with me much as in the beginning. I would know that nothing had changed, that a little resolution is all that is needed to come and go under the changing sky, on the moving earth, as all along the long summer days too short for all the play, it was known as play, if my head could think. The air would be there again, the shadows of the sky drifting over the earth, and that ant, that ant, oh most excellent head that can't think. Leave it, leave it, nothing leads to anything, nothing of all that, my life is varied, you can't have everything, I'll never get anywhere, but when did I? When I laboured, all day long and let me add, before I forget, part of the night, when I thought that with perseverance I'd get at me in the end? Well look at me, a little dust in a little nook, stirred faintly this way and that by breath straying from the lost without. Yes, I'm here for ever, with the spinners and the dead flies, dancing to the tremor of their meshed wings, and it's well pleased I am, well pleased, that it's over and done with, the puffing and panting after me up and down their Tempe of tears. Sometimes a butterfly comes, all warm from the flowers, how weak it is, and quick dead, the wings crosswise, as when resting, in the sun, the scales grey. Blot, words can be blotted and the mad thoughts they invent, the nostalgia for that slime where the Eternal breathed and his son wrote, long after, with divine idiotic finger, at the feet of the adulteress, wipe it out, all you have to do is say you said nothing and so say nothing again. What can have become then of the tissues I was, I can see them no more, feel them no more, flaunting and fluttering all about and inside me, pah they must be still on their old prowl somewhere, passing themselves off as me. Did I ever believe in them, did I ever believe I was there, somewhere in that ragbag, that's more the line, of inquiry, perhaps I'm still there, as large as life, merely convinced I'm not. The eyes, yes, if these memories are mine, I must have believed in them an instant, believed it was me I saw there dimly in the depths of their glades. I can see me still, with those of now, sealed this long time, staring with those of then, I must have been twelve, because of the glass, a round shaving-glass, double-faced, faithful and magnifying, staring into one of the others, the true ones, true then, and seeing me there, imagining I saw me there, lurking behind the bluey veils, staring back sightlessly, at the age of twelve, because of the glass, on its pivot, because of my father, if it was my father, in the bathroom, with its view of the sea, the lightships at night, the red harbour light, if these memories concern me, at the age of twelve, or at the age of forty, for the mirror remained, my father went but the mirror remained, in which he had so greatly changed, my mother did her hair in it, with twitching hands, in another house, with no view of the sea, with a view of the mountains, if it was my mother, what a refreshing whiff of life on earth. I was, I was, they say in Purgatory, in Hell too, admirable singulars, admirable assurance. Plunged in ice up to the nostrils, the eyelids caked with frozen tears, to fight all your battles o'er again, what tranquillity, and know there are no more emotions in store, no, I can't have heard aright. How many hours to go, before the next silence, they are not hours, it will not be silence, how many hours still, before the next silence? Ah to know for sure, to know that this thing has no end, this thing, this thing, this farrago of silence and words, of silence that is not silence and barely murmured words. Or to know it's life still, a form of life, ordained to end, as others ended and will end, till life ends, in all its forms. Words, mine was never more than that, than this pell-mell babel of silence and words, my viewless form described as ended, or to come, or still in progress, depending on the words, the moments, long may it last in that singular way. Apparitions, keepers, what childishness, and ghouls, to think I said ghouls, do I as much as know what they are, of course I don't, and how the intervals are filled, as if I didn't know, as if there were two things, some other thing besides this thing, what is it, this unnamable thing that I name and name and never wear out, and I call that words. It's because I haven't hit on the right ones, the killers, haven't yet heaved them up from that heart-burning glut of words, with what words shall I name my unnamable words? And yet I have high hopes, I give you my word, high hopes, that one day I may tell a story, hear a story, yet another, with men, kinds of men as in the days when I played all regardless or nearly, worked and played. But first stop talking and get on with your weeping, with eyes wide open that the precious liquid may spill freely, without burning the lids, or the crystalline humour, I forget, whatever it is it burns. Tears, that could be the tone, if they weren't so easy, the true tone and tenor at last. Besides not a tear, not one, I'd be in greater danger of mirth, if it wasn't so easy. No, grave, I'll be grave, I'll close my ears, close my mouth and be grave. And when they open again it may be to hear a story, tell a story, in the true sense of the words, the word hear, the word tell, the word story, I have high hopes, a little story, with living creatures coming and going on a habitable earth crammed with the dead, a brief story, with night and day coming and going above, if they stretch that far, the words that remain, and I've high hopes, I give you my word.

7

Did I try everything, ferret in every hold, secretly, silently, patiently, listening? I'm in earnest, as so often, I'd like to be sure I left no stone unturned before reporting me missing and giving up. In every hold, I mean in all those places where there was a chance of my being, where once I used to lurk, waiting for the hour to come when I might venture forth, tried and trusty places, that's all I meant when I said in every hold. Once, I mean in the days when I still could move, and feel myself moving, painfully, barely, but unquestionably changing position on the whole, the trees were witness, the sands, the air of the heights, the cobblestones. This tone is promising, it is more like that of old, of the days and nights when in spite of all I was calm, treading back and forth the futile road, knowing it short and easy seen from Sirius, and deadly calm at the heart of my frenzies. My question, I had a question, ah yes, did I try everything, I can see it still, but it's passing, lighter than air, like a cloud, in moonlight, before the skylight, before the moon, like the moon, before the skylight. No, in its own way, I know it well, the way of an evening shadow you follow with your eyes, thinking of something else, yes, that's it, the mind elsewhere, and the eyes too, if the truth were known, the eyes elsewhere too. Ah if there must be speech at least none from the heart, no, I have only one desire, if I have it still. But another thing, before the ones that matter, I have just time, if I make haste, in the trough of all this time just time. Another thing, I call that another thing, the old thing I keep on not saying till I'm sick and tired, revelling in the flying instants, I call that revelling, now's my chance and I talk of revelling, it won't come back in a hurry if I remember right, but come back it must with its riot of instants. It's not me in any case, I'm not talking of me, I've said it a million times, no point in apologizing again, for talking of me, when there's X, that paradigm of human kind, moving at will, complete with joys and sorrows, perhaps even a wife and brats, forbears most certainly, a carcass in God's image and a contemporary skull, but above all endowed with movement, that's what strikes you above all, with his likeness so easy to take and his so instructive soul, that really, no, to talk of oneself, when there's X, no, what a blessing I'm not talking of myself, enough vile parrot I'll kill you. And what if all this time I had not stirred hand or foot from the third class waiting-room of the South-Eastern Railway Terminus, I never dared wait first on a third-class ticket, and were still there waiting to leave, for the south-east, the south rather, east lay the sea, all along the track, wondering where on earth to alight, or my mind absent, elsewhere. The last train went at twenty-three thirty, then they closed the station for the night. What thronging memories, that's to make me think I'm dead, I've said it a million times. But the same return, like the spokes of a turning wheel, always the same, and all alike, like spokes. And yet I wonder, whenever the hour returns when I have to

ARIKHA 57

wonder that, if the wheel in my head turns, I wonder, so given am I to thinking with my blood, or if it merely swings, like a balance-wheel in its case, a minute to and fro, seeing the immensity to measure and that heads are only wound up once, so given am I to thinking with my breath. But tut there I am far again from that terminus and its pretty neo-Doric colonnade, and far from that heap of flesh, rind, bones and bristles waiting to depart it knows not where, somewhere south, perhaps asleep, its ticket between finger and thumb for the sake of appearances, or let fall to the ground in the great limpness of sleep, perhaps dreaming it's in heaven, alit in heaven, or better still the dawn, waiting for the dawn and the joy of being able to say, I've the whole day before me, to go wrong, to go right, to calm down, to give up, I've nothing to fear, my ticket is valid for life. Is it there I came to a stop, is that me still waiting there, sitting up stiff and straight on the edge of the seat, knowing the dangers of laisser-aller, hands on thighs, ticket between finger and thumb, in that great room dim with the platform gloom as dispensed by the quarter-glass self-closing door, locked up in those shadows, it's there, it's me. In that case the night is long and singularly silent, for one who seems to remember the city sounds, confusedly, sunk now to a single sound, the impossible confused memory of a single confused sound, lasting all night, swelling, dying, but never for an instant broken by a silence the like of this deafening silence. Whence it should follow, but does not, that the third class waiting-room of the South-Eastern Railway Terminus must be struck from the list of places to visit, see above, centuries above, that this lump is no longer me and that search should be made elsewhere, unless it be abandoned, which is my feeling. But not so fast, all cities are not eternal, that of this pensum is perhaps among the dead, and the station in ruins where I sit waiting, erect and rigid, hands on thighs, the tip of the ticket between finger and thumb, for a train that will never come, never go, natureward, or for day to break behind the locked door, through the glass black with the dust of ruin. That is why one must not hasten to conclude, the risk of error is too great. And to search for me elsewhere, where life persists, and me there, whence all life has withdrawn, except mine, if I'm alive, no, it would be a loss of time. And personally, I hear it said, personally I have no more time to lose, and that that will be all for this evening, that night is at hand and the time come for me too to begin.

8

Only the words break the silence, all other sounds have ceased. If I were silent I'd hear nothing. But if I were silent the other sounds would start again, those to which the words have made me deaf, or which have really ceased. But I am silent, it sometimes happens, no, never, not one second. I weep too without interruption. It's an unbroken flow of words and tears. With no pause for reflection. But I speak softer, every year a little softer. Perhaps. Slower too, every year a little slower. Perhaps. It is hard for me to judge. If so the pauses would be longer, between the words, the sentences, the syllables, the tears, I confuse them, words and tears, my words are my tears, my eyes my mouth. And I should hear, at every little pause, if it's the silence I say when I say that only the words break it. But nothing of the kind, that's not how it is, it's for ever the same murmur, flowing unbroken, like a single endless word and therefore meaningless, for it's the end gives the meaning to words. What right have you then, no, this time I see what I'm up to and put a stop to it, saying, None, none. But get on with the stupid old threne and ask, ask until you answer, a new question, the most ancient of all, the question were things always so. Well I'm going to tell myself something (if I'm able), pregnant I hope with promise for the future, namely that I begin to have no very clear recollection of how things were before (I was!), and by before I mean elsewhere, time has turned into space and there will be no more time, till I get out of here. Yes, my past has thrown me out, its gates have slammed behind me, or I burrowed my way out alone, to linger a moment free in a dream of days and nights, dreaming of me moving, season after season, towards the last, like the living, till suddenly I was here, all memory gone. Ever since nothing but fantasies and hope of a story for me somehow, of having come from somewhere and of being able to go back, or on, somehow, some day, or without hope. Without what hope, haven't I just said, of seeing me alive, not merely inside an imaginary head, but a pebble sand to be, under a restless sky, restless on its shore, faint stirs day and night, as if to grow less could help, ever less and less and never quite be gone. No truly, no matter what, I say no matter what, hoping to wear out a voice, to wear out a head, or without hope, without reason, no matter what, without reason. But it will end, a desinence will come, or the breath fail better still, I'll be silence, I'll know I'm silence, no, in the silence you can't know, I'll never know anything. But at least get out of here, at least that, no? I don't know. And time begin again, the steps on the earth, the night the fool implores at morning and the morning he begs at evening not to dawn. I don't know, I don't know what all that means, day and night, earth and sky, begging and imploring. And I can desire them? Who says I desire them, the voice, and that I can't desire anything, that looks like a contradiction, it may be for all I know. Me, here, if they could open, those little words, open and swallow me up, perhaps that is what has happened. If so let them open again and let me out, in the tumult of light that sealed my eyes, and of men, to try and be one again. Or if I'm guilty let me be forgiven and graciously authorized to expiate, coming and going in passing time, every day a little purer, a little deader. The mistake I make is to try and think, even the way I do, such as I am I shouldn't be able, even the way I do. But whom can I have offended so grievously, to be punished in this inexplicable way, all is inexplicable, space and time, false and inexplicable, suffering and tears, and even the old convulsive cry, It's not me, it can't be me. But am I in pain, whether it's me or not, frankly now, is there pain? Now is here and here there is no frankness, all I say will be false and to begin with not said by me, here I'm a mere ventriloquist's dummy, I feel nothing, say nothing, he holds me in his arms and moves my lips with a string, with a fish-hook, no, no need of lips, all is dark, there is no one, what's the matter with my head, I must have left it in Ireland, in a saloon, it must be there still, lying on the bar, it's all it deserved. But that other who is me, blind and deaf and mute, because of whom I'm here, in this black silence, helpless to move or accept this voice as mine, it's as him I must disguise myself till I die, for him in the meantime do my best not to live, in this pseudo-sepulture claiming to be his. Whereas to my certain knowledge I'm dead and kicking above, somewhere in Europe probably, with every plunge and suck of the sky a little more overripe, as yesterday in the pump of the womb. No, to have said so convinces me of the contrary, I never saw the light of day, any more than he, ah if no were content to cut yes's throat and never cut its own. Watch out for the right moment, then not another word, is that the only way to have being and habitat? But I'm here, that much at least is certain, it's in vain I keep on saying it, it remains true. Does it? It's hard for me to judge. Less true and less certain in any case than when I say I'm on earth, come into the world and assured of getting out, that's why I say it, patiently, variously, trying to vary, for you never know, it's perhaps all a question of hitting on the right aggregate. So as to be here no more at last, to have never been here, but all this time above, with a name like a dog to be called up with and distinctive marks to be had up with, the chest expanding and contracting unaided, panting towards the grand apnoea. The right aggregate, but there are four million possible, nay probable, according to Aristotle, who knew everything. But what is this I see, and how, a white stick and an ear-trumpet, where, Place de la République, at pernod time, let me look closer at this, it's perhaps me at last. The trumpet, sailing at ear level, suddenly resembles a steam-whistle, of the kind thanks to which my steamers forge fearfully through the fog. That should fix the period, to the nearest half-century or so. The stick gains ground, tapping with its ferrule the noble bassamento of the United Stores, it must be winter, at least not summer. I can also just discern, with a final effort of will, a bowler hat which seems to my sorrow a sardonic synthesis of all those that never fitted me and, at the other extremity, similarly suspicious, a complete pair of brown boots lacerated and gaping. These insignia, if I may so describe them, advance in concert, as though connected by the traditional human excipient, halt, move on again, confirmed by the vast show windows. The level of the hat, and consequently of the trumpet, hold out some hope for me as a dying dwarf or at least hunchback. The vacancy is tempting, shall I enthrone my infirmities, give them this chance again, my dream infirmities, that they may take flesh and move, deteriorating, round and round this grandiose square which I hope I don't confuse with the Bastille, until they are deemed worthy of the adjacent Père Lachaise or, better still, prematurely relieved trying to cross over, at the hour of night's young thoughts. No, the answer is no. For even as I moved, or when the moment came, affecting beyond all others, to hold out my hand, or hat, without previous song, or any other form of concession to self-respect, at the terrace of a café, or in the mouth of the underground, I would know it was not me, I would know I was here, begging in another dark, another silence, for another alm, that of being or of ceasing, better still, before having been. And the hand old in vain would drop the mite and the old feet shuffle on, towards an even vainer death than no matter whose.

9

If I said, There's a way out there, there's a way out somewhere, the rest would come. What am I waiting for then, to say it? To believe it? And what does that mean, the rest? Shall I answer, try and answer, or go on as though I had asked nothing? I don't know, I can't know beforehand, nor after, nor during, the future will tell, some future instant, soon, or late, I won't hear, I won't understand, all dies so fast, no sooner born. And the yeses and noes mean nothing in this mouth, no more than sighs it sighs in its toil, or answers to a question not understood, a question unspoken, in the eyes of a mute, an idiot, who doesn't understand, never understood, who stares at himself in a glass, stares before him in the desert, sighing yes, sighing no, on and off. But there is reasoning somewhere, moments of reasoning, that is to say the same things recur, they drive one another out, they draw one another back, no need to know what things. It's mechanical, like the great colds, the great heats, the long days, the long nights, of the moon, such is my conviction, for I have convictions, when their turn comes round, then stop having them, that's how it goes, it must be supposed, at least it must be said, since I have just said it. The way out, this evening it's the turn of the way out, isn't it like a duo, or a trio, yes, there are moments when it's like that, then they pass and it's not like that any more, never was like that, is like nothing, no resemblance with anything, of no interest. What variety and at the same time what monotony, how varied it is and at the same time how, what's the word, how monotonous. What agitation and at the same time what calm, what vicissitudes within what changelessness. Moments of hesitation not so much rare as frequent, if one had to choose, and soon overcome in favour of the old crux, on which at first all depends, then much, then little, then nothing. That's right, wordshit, bury me, avalanche, and let there be no more talk of any creature, nor of a world to leave, nor of a world to reach, in order to have done, with worlds, with creatures, with words, with misery, misery. Which no sooner said, Ah, says I, punctually, if only I could say, There's a way out there, there's a way out somewhere, then all would be said, it would be the first step on the long travelable road, destination tomb, to be trod without a word, tramp tramp, little heavy irrevocable steps, down the long tunnels at first, then under the mortal skies, through the days and nights, faster and faster, no, slower and slower, for obvious reasons, and at the same time faster and faster, for other obvious reasons, or the same, obvious in a different way, or in the same way, but at a different moment of time, a moment earlier, a moment later, or at the same moment, there is no such thing, there would be no such thing, I recapitulate, impossible. Would I know where I came from, no, I'd have a mother, I'd have had a mother, and what I came out of, with what pain, no, I'd have forgotten, what is it makes me say that, what is it makes me say this, whatever it is makes me say all,

and it's not certain, not certain the way the mother would be certain, the way the tomb would be certain, if there was a way out, if I said there was a way out, make me say it, demons, no, I'll ask for nothing. Yes, I'd have a mother, I'd have a tomb, I wouldn't have come out of here, one doesn't come out of here, here are my tomb and mother, it's all here this evening, I'm dead and getting born, without having ended, helpless to begin, that's my life. How reasonable it is and what am I complaining of? Is it because I'm no longer slinking to and fro before the graveyard, saying, God grant I'm buriable before the curtain drops, is that my grievance, it's possible. I was well inspired to be anxious, wondering on what score, and I asked myself, as I came and went, on what score I could possibly be anxious, and found the answer and answered, saying, It's not me, I haven't yet appeared, I haven't yet been noticed, and saying further, Oh yes it is, it's me all right, and ceasing to be what is more, then quickening my step, so as to arrive before the next onslaught, as though it were on time I trod, and saying further, and so forth. I can scarcely have gone unperceived, all this time, and yet you wouldn't have thought so, that I didn't go unperceived. I don't refer to the spoken salutation, I'd have been the first to be perturbed by that, almost as much as by the bow, kiss or handshake. But the other signs, irrepressible, with which the fellow-creature unwillingly betrays your presence, the shudders and wry faces, nothing of that nature either it would seem, except possibly on the part of certain hearse-horses, in spite of their blinkers and strict funereal training, but perhaps I flatter myself. Truly I can't recall a single face, proof positive that I was not there, no, proof of nothing. But the fact that I was not molested, can I have remained insensible to that? Alas I fear they could have subjected me to the most gratifying brutalities, I won't go so far as to say without my knowledge, but without my being encouraged, as a result, to feel myself there rather than elsewhere. And I may well have spent one half of my life in the prisons of their Arcady, purging the delinquencies of the other half, all unaware of any break or lull in my problematic patrolling, unconstrained, before the gates of the graveyard. But what if weary of seeing me relieve myself, of seeing me resume, after each forced vacation, my beat before the gates of the graveyard, what if finally they had plucked up heart and slightly stressed their blows, just enough to confer death, without any mutilation of the corpse, there, at the gates of the graveyard, where that very morning I had reappeared, no sooner set at large, and resumed by old offence, to and fro, with step now slow and now precipitate, like that of the conspirator Catilina plotting the ruin of the fatherland, saying, It's not me, yes, it's me, and further, There's a way out there, no no, I'm getting mixed, I must be getting mixed, confusing here and there, now and then, just as I confused them then, the here of then, the then of there, with other spaces, other times, dimly discerned, but not more dimly than now, now that I'm here, if I'm here, and no longer there, coming and going before the graveyard, perplexed. Or did I end up by simply sitting down, with my back to the wall, all the long night before me when the dead lie waiting, on the beds where they died, shrouded or coffined, for the sun to rise? What am I doing now, I'm trying to see where I am, so as to be able to go elsewhere, should occasion arise, or else simply to say, You have merely to wait till they come and fetch you, that's my impression at times. Then it goes and I see it's not that, but something else, difficult to grasp, and which I don't grasp, or which I do grasp, it depends, and it comes to the same, for it's not that either, but something else, some other thing, or the first back again, or still the same, always the same thing proposing itself to my perplexity, then disappearing, then proposing itself again, to my perplexity still unsated, or momentarily dead, of starvation. The graveyard, yes, it's there I'd return, this evening it's there, borne by my words, if I could get out of here, that is to say if I could say, There's a way out there, there's a way out somewhere, to know exactly where would be a mere matter of time, and patience, and sequency of thought, and felicity of expression. But the body, to get there with, where's the body? It's a minor point, a minor point. And I have no doubts, I'd get there somehow, to the way out, sooner or later, if I could say, There's a way out there, there's a way out somewhere, the rest would come, the other words, sooner or later, and the power to get there, and the way to get there, and pass out, and see the beauties of the skies, and see the stars again.

10

Give up, but it's all given up, it's nothing new, I'm nothing new. Ah so there was something once, I had something once. It may be thought there was, so long as it's known there was not, never anything, but giving up. But let us suppose there was not, that is to say let us suppose there was, something once, in a head, in a heart, in a hand, before all opened, emptied, shut again and froze. This is most reassuring, after such a fright, and emboldens me to go on, once again. But there is not silence. No, there is utterance, somewhere someone is uttering. Inanities, agreed, but is that enough, is that enough, to make sense? I see what it is, the head has fallen behind, all the rest has gone on, the head and its anus the mouth, or else it has gone on alone, all alone on its old prowls, slobbering its shit and lapping it back off the lips like in the days when it fancied itself. But the heart's not in it any more, nor is the appetite what it was. So home to roost it comes among my other assets, home yet again, and no trickery involved, that old past ever new, ever ended, ever ending, with all its hidden treasures of promise for tomorrow, and of consolation for today. And I'm in good hands again, they hold my head from behind, intriguing detail, as at the hairdresser's, the forefingers close my eyes, the middle fingers my nostrils, the thumbs stop up my ears, but imperfectly, to enable me to hear, but imperfectly, while the four remaining busy themselves with my jaws and tongue, to enable me to suffocate, but imperfectly, and to utter, for my good, what I must utter, for my future good, well-known ditty, and in particular to observe without delay, speaking of the passing moment, that worse have been known to pass, that it will pass in time, a mere moment of respite which but for this first aid might have proved fatal, and that one day I shall know again that I once was, and roughly who, and how to go on, and speak unaided, nicely, about number one and his pale imitations. And it is possible, just, for I must not be too affirmative at this stage, it would not be in my interest, that other fingers, quite a different gang, other tentacles, that's more like it, other charitable suckers, waste no more time trying to get it right, will take down my declarations, so that at the close of the interminable delirium, should it ever resume, I may not be reproached with having faltered. This is awful, awful, at least there's that to be thankful for. And perhaps beside me, and all around, other souls are being licked into shape, souls swooned away, or sick with over-use, or because no use could be found for them, but still fit for use, or fit only to be cast away, pale imitations of mine. Or has it knelled here at last for our committal to flesh, as the dead are committed to the ground, in the hour of their death at last, and at the place where they die, to keep the expenses down, or for our reassignment, souls of the stillborn, or dead before the body, or still young in the midst of the ruins, or never come to life through incapacity or for some other reason, or the immortal type, there must be a few of them too, whose bodies were always wrong, but patience there's a true one in pickle, among the unborn hordes, the true sepulchral body, for the living have no room for a second. No, no souls, or bodies, or birth, or life, or death, you've got to go on without any of that junk, that's all dead with words, with excess of words, they can say nothing else, they say there is nothing else, that here it's that and nothing else, but they won't say it eternally, they'll find some other nonsense, no matter what, and I'll be able to go on, no, I'll be able to stop, or start, another guzzle of lies but piping hot, it will last my time, it will be my time and place, my voice and silence, a voice of silence, the voice of my silence. It's with such prospects they exhort you to have patience, whereas you are patient, and calm, somehow somewhere calm, what calm here, ah that's an idea, say how calm it is here, and how fine I feel, and how silent I am, I'll start right away, I'll say what calm and silence, which nothing has ever broken, nothing will ever break, which saying I don't break, or saying I'll be saying, yes, I'll say all that tomorrow, yes, tomorrow evening, some other evening, not this evening, this evening it's too late, too late to get things right, I'll go to sleep, so that I may say, hear myself say, a little later, I've slept, he's slept, but he won't have slept, or else he's sleeping now, he'll have done nothing, nothing but go on, doing what, doing what he does, that is to say, I don't know, giving up, that's it, I'll have gone on giving up, having had nothing, not being there.

11

When I think, no, that won't work, when come those who knew me, perhaps even know me still, by sight of course, or by smell, it's as though, it's as if, come on, I don't know, I shouldn't have begun. If I began again, setting my mind to it, that sometimes gives good results, it's worth trying, I'll try it, one of these days, one of these evenings, or this evening, why not this evening, before I disappear, from up there, from down here, scattered by the everlasting words. What am I saying, scattered, isn't that just what I'm not, just what I'm not, I was wandering, my mind was wandering, just the very thing I'm not. And it's still the same old road I'm trudging, up yes and down no, towards one yet to be named, so that he may leave me in peace, be in peace, be no more, have never been. Name, no, nothing is namable, tell, no, nothing can be told, what then, I don't know, I shouldn't have begun. Add him to the repertory, there we have it, and execute him, as I execute me, one dead bar after another, evening after evening, and night after night, and all through the days, but it's always evening, why is that, why is it always evening, I'll say why, so as to have said it, have it behind me, an instant. It's time that can't go on at the hour of the serenade, unless it's dawn, no, I'm not in the open, I'm under the ground, or in my body somewhere, or in another body, and time devours on, but not me, there we have it, that's why it's always evening, to let me have the best to look forward to, the long black night to sleep in, there, I've answered, I've answered something. Or it's in the head, like a minute time switch, a second time switch, or it's like a patch of sea, under the passing lighthouse beam, a passing patch of sea under the passing beam. Vile words to make me believe I'm here, and that I have a head, and a voice, a head believing this, then that, then nothing more, neither in itself, nor in anything else, but a head with a voice belonging to it, or to others, other heads, as if there were two heads, as if there were one head, or headless, a headless voice, but a voice. But I'm not deceived, for the moment I'm not deceived, for the moment I'm not there, nor anywhere else what is more, neither as head, nor as voice, nor as testicle, what a shame, what a shame I'm not appearing anywhere as testicle, or as cunt, those areas, a female pubic hair, it sees great sights, peeping down, well, there it is, can't be helped, that's how it is. And I let them say their say, my words not said by me, me that word, that word they say, but say in vain. We're getting on, getting on, and when come those who knew me, quick quick, it's as though, no, premature. But peekaboo here I come again, just when most needed, like the square root of minus one, having terminated my humanities, this should be worth seeing, the livid face stained with ink and jam, caput mortuum of a studious youth, ears akimbo, eyes back to front, the odd stray hair, foaming at the mouth, and chewing, what is it chewing, a gob, a prayer, a lesson, a little of each, a prayer got by rote in case of emergency before the soul resigns and bubbling up all arsy-varsy in the old mouth bereft of words, in the old head done with listening, there I am old, it doesn't take long, a snotty old nipper, having terminated his humanities, in the two-stander urinal on the corner of the Rue d'Assas was it, with the leak making the same gurgle as sixty years ago, my favourite because of the encouragement like mother hissing to baby on pot, my brow glued to the partition among the graffiti, straining against the prostate, belching up Hail Marys, buttoned as to the fly, I invent nothing, through absent-mindedness, or exhaustion, or insouciance, or on purpose, to promote priming, I know what I mean, or one-armed better still, no arms, no hands, better by far, as old as the world and no less hideous, amputated on all sides, erect on my trusty stumps, bursting with old piss, old prayers, old lessons, soul, mind and carcass finishing neck and neck, not to mention the gobchucks, too painful to mention, sobs made mucus, hawked up from the heart, now I have a heart, now I'm complete, apart from a few extremities, having terminated their humanities, then their career, and with that not in the least pretentious, making no demands, rent with ejaculations, Jesus, Jesus. Evenings, evenings, what evenings they were then, made of what, and when was that, I don't know, made of friendly shadows, friendly skies, of time cloyed, resting from devouring, until its midnight meats, I don't know, any more than then, when I used to say, from within, or from without, from the coming night or from under the ground, Where am I, to mention only space, and in what semblance, and since when, to mention also time, and till when, and who is this clot who doesn't know where to go, who can't stop, who takes himself for me and for whom I take myself, anything at all, the old jangle. Those evenings then, but what is this evening made of, this evening now that never ends, in whose shadows I'm alone, that's where I am, where I was then, where I've always been, it's from them I spoke to myself, spoke to him, where has he vanished, the one I saw then, is he still in the street, it's probable, it's possible, with no voice speaking to him, I don't speak to him any more, I don't speak to me any more, I have no one left to speak to, and I speak, a voice speaks that can be none but mine, since there is none but me. Yes, I have lost him and he has lost me, lost from view, lost from hearing, that's what I wanted, is it possible, that I wanted that, wanted this, and he, what did he want, he wanted to stop, perhaps he has stopped, I have stopped, but I never stirred, perhaps he is dead, I am dead, but I never lived. But he moved, proof of animation, through those evenings, moving too, evenings with an end, evenings with a night, never saying a word, unable to say a word, not knowing where to go, unable to stop, listening to my cries, hearing a voice crying that it was no kind of life, as if he didn't know, as if the allusion was to his, which was a kind of one, there's the difference, those were the days, I didn't know where I was, nor in what semblance, nor since when, nor till when, whereas now, there's the difference, now I know, it's not true, but I say it just the same, there's the difference, I'm saying it now, I'll say it soon, I'll say it in the end, then end, I'll be free to end, I won't be any more, it won't be worth it any more, it won't be necessary any more, it won't be possible any more, but it's not worth it now, it's not necessary now, it's not possible now, that's how the reasoning runs. No, something better must be found, a better reason, for this to stop, another word, a better idea, to put in the negative, a new no, to cancel all the others, all the old noes that buried me down here, deep in this place which is not one, which is merely a moment for the time being eternal, which is called here, and in this being which is called me and is not one, and in this impossible voice, all the old noes dangling in the dark and swaying like a ladder of smoke, yes, a new no, that none says twice, whose drop will fall and let me down, shadow and babble, to an absence less vain than inexistence. Oh I know it won't happen like that, I know that nothing will happen, that nothing has happened and that I'm still, and particularly since the day I could no longer believe it, what is called flesh and blood somewhere above in their gonorrhoeal light, cursing myself heartily. And that is why, when comes the hour of those who knew me, this time it's going to work, when comes the hour of those who knew me, it's as though I were among them, that is what I had to say, among them watching me approach, then watching me recede, shaking my head and saying, Is it really he, can it possibly be he, then moving on in their company along a road that is not mine and with every step takes me further from that other not mine either, or remaining alone where I am, between two parting dreams, knowing none, known of none, that finally is what I had to say, that is all I can have had to say, this evening.

12

It's a winter night, where I was, where I'm going, remembered, imagined, no matter, believing in me, believing it's me, no, no need, so long as the others are there, where, in the world of the others, of the long mortal ways, under the sky, with a voice, no, no need, and the power to move, now and then, no need either, so long as the others move, the true others, but on earth, beyond all doubt on earth, for as long as it takes to die again, wake again, long enough for things to change here, for something to change, to make possible a deeper birth, a deeper death, or resurrection in and out of this murmur of memory and dream. A winter night, without moon or stars, but light, he sees his body, all the front, part of the front, what makes them light, this impossible night, this impossible body, it's me in him remembering, remembering the true night, dreaming of the night without morning, and how will he manage tomorrow, to endure tomorrow, the dawning, then the day, the same as he managed yesterday, to endure yesterday. Oh I know, it's not me, not yet, it's a veteran, inured to days and nights, but he forgets, he thinks of me, more than is wise, and it's a far cry to morning, perhaps it has time never to dawn at last. That's what he says, with his voice soon to leave him, perhaps tonight, and he says, How light it is, how shall I manage tomorrow, how did I manage yesterday, pah it's the end, it's a far cry to morning, and who's this speaking in me, and who's this disowning me, as though I had taken his place, usurped his life, that old shame that kept me from living, the shame of my living that kept me from living, and so on, muttering, the old inanities, his chin on his heart, his arms dangling, sagging at the knees, in the night. Will they succeed in slipping me into him, the memory and dream of me, into him still living, amn't I there already, wasn't I always there, like a stain of remorse, is that my night and contumacy, in the dungeons of this moribund, and from now till he dies my last chance to have been, and who is this raving now, pah there are voices everywhere, ears everywhere, one who speaks saying, without ceasing to speak, Who's speaking?, and one who hears, mute, uncomprehending, far from all, and bodies everywhere, bent, fixed, where my prospects must be just as good, just as poor, as in this firstcomer. And none will wait, he no more than the others, none ever waited to die for me to live in him, so as to die with him, but quick quick all die, saying, Quick quick let us die, without him, as we lived, before it's too late, lest we won't have lived. And this other now, obviously, what's to be said of this latest other, with his babble of homeless mes and untenanted hims, this other without number or person whose abandoned being we haunt, nothing. There's a pretty three in one, and what a one, what a no one. So, I'm supposed to say now, it's the moment, so that's the earth, these expiring vitals set aside for me which no sooner taken over would be set aside for another, many thanks, and here the laugh, the long silent guffaw of the knowing non-exister, at hearing ascribed to him such pregnant words, confess you're not the man you were, you'll end up riding a bicycle. That's the accountants' chorus, opining like a single man, and there are more to come, all the peoples of the earth would not suffice, at the end of the billions you'd need a god, unwitnessed witness of witnesses, what a blessing it's all down the drain, nothing ever as much as begun, nothing ever but nothing and never, nothing ever but lifeless words.

13

Weaker still the weak old voice that tried in vain to make me, dying away as much as to say it's going from here to try elsewhere, or dying down, there's no telling, as much as to say it's going to cease, give up trying. No voice ever but it in my life, it says, if speaking of me one can speak of life, and it can, it still can, or if not of life, there it dies, if this, if that, if speaking of me, there it dies, but who can the greater can the less, once you've spoken of me you can speak of anything, up to the point where, up to the time when, there it dies, it can't go on, it's been its death, speaking of me, here or elsewhere, it says, it murmurs. Whose voice, no one's, there is no one, there's a voice without a mouth, and somewhere a kind of hearing, something compelled to hear, and somewhere a hand, it calls that a hand, it wants to make a hand, or if not a hand something somewhere that can leave a trace, of what is made, of what is said, you can't do with less, no, that's romancing, more romancing, there is nothing but a voice murmuring a trace. A trace, it wants to leave a trace, yes, like air leaves among the leaves, among the grass, among the sand, it's with that it would make a life, but soon it will be the end, it won't be long now, there won't be any life, there won't have been any life, there will be silence, the air quite still that trembled once an instant, the tiny flurry of dust quite settled. Air, dust, there is no air here, nor anything to make dust, and to speak of instants, to speak of once, is to speak of nothing, but there it is, those are the expressions it employs. It has always spoken, it will always speak, of things that don't exist, or only exist elsewhere, if you like, if you must, if that may be called existing. Unfortunately it is not a question of elsewhere, but of here, ah there are the words out at last, out again, that was the only chance, get out of here and go elsewhere, go where time passes and atoms assemble an instant, where the voice belongs perhaps, where it sometimes says it must have belonged, to be able to speak of such figments. Yes, out of here, but how when here is empty, not a speck of dust, not a breath, the voice's breath alone, it breathes in vain, nothing is made. If I were here, if it could have made me, how I would pity it, for having spoken so long in vain, no, that won't do, it wouldn't have spoken in vain if I were here, and I wouldn't pity it if it had made me, I'd curse it, or bless it, it would be in my mouth, cursing, blessing, whom, what, it wouldn't be able to say, in my mouth it wouldn't have much to say, that had so much to say in vain. But this pity, all the same, it wonders, this pity that is in the air, though no air here for pity, but it's the expression, it wonders should it stop and wonder what pity is doing here and if it's not hope gleaming, another expression, evilly among the imaginary ashes, the faint hope of a faint being after all, human in kind, tears in its eyes before they've had time to open, no, no more stopping and wondering, about that or anything else, nothing will stop it any more, in its fall, or in its rise, perhaps it will end on a castrato scream. True there was never much talk of the heart, literal or figurative, but that's no reason for hoping, what, that one day there will be one, to send up above to break in the galanty show, pity. But what more is it waiting for now, when there's no doubt left, no choice left, to stick a sock in its death-rattle, yet another locution. To have rounded off its cock-and-bullshit in a coda worthy of the rest? Last everlasting questions, infant languors in the end sheets, last images, end of dream, of being past, passing and to be, end of lie. Is it possible, is that the possible thing at last, the extinction of this black nothing and its impossible shades, the end of the farce of making and the silencing of silence, it wonders, that voice which is silence, or it's me, there's no telling, it's all the same dream, the same silence, it and me, it and him, him and me, and all our train, and all theirs, and all theirs, but whose, whose dream, whose silence, old questions, last questions, ours who are dream and silence, but it's ended, we're ended who never were, soon there will be nothing where there was never anything, last images. And whose the shame, at every mute micromillisyllable, and unslakable infinity of remorse delving ever deeper in its bite, at having to hear, having to say, fainter than the faintest murmur, so many lies, so many times the same lie lyingly denied, whose the screaming silence of no's knife in yes's wound, it wonders. And wonders what has become of the wish to know, it is gone, the heart is gone, the head is gone, no one feels anything, asks anything, seeks anything, says anything, hears anything, there is only silence. It's not true, yes, it's true, it's true and it's not true, there is silence and there is not silence, there is no one and there is someone, nothing prevents anything. And were the voice to cease quite at last, the old ceasing voice, it would not be true, as it is not true that it speaks, it can't speak, it can't cease. And were there one day to be here, where there are no days, which is no place, born of the impossible voice the unmakable being, and a gleam of light, still all would be silent and empty and dark, as now, as soon now, when all will be ended, all said, it says, it murmurs.